THE FORGOTTEN AND THE FANTASTICAL

Also by Teika Bellamy

<u>Editor</u>:

Musings on Mothering (Mother's Milk Books 2012)

Letting Go by Angela Topping (Mother's Milk Books 2013)

Look At All The Women by Cathy Bryant (Mother's Milk Books 2014)

The Mother's Milk Books Writing Prize Anthology 2013: PARENTING (Mother's Milk Books 2014)

THE FORGOTTEN AND THE FANTASTICAL

Modern fables and ancient tales

EDITED BY TEIKA BELLAMY

Mother's Milk Books

First published in Great Britain in 2015 by Mother's Milk Books

Front cover image 'Lady Seaweed' copyright © Marija Smits 2014
Cover design copyright © Teika Bellamy 2015
Introduction copyright © Teika Bellamy 2015
Illustrations copyright © Marija Smits 2015

ISBN 978-0-9573858-4-9

Typeset in Georgia and Lt Oksana by Teika Bellamy.
Lt Oksana font designed by Lauren Thompson.
Printed and bound in Great Britain by The Russell Press, Nottingham,
on FSC paper and board sourced from sustainable forests.
www.russellpress.com

First published in 2015 by Mother's Milk Books
www.mothersmilkbooks.com

SPECIAL THANKS TO:

All the wonderful writers who trusted me with their
precious stories, and of course to my husband, Tom,
who continues to provide me with inspiration and support.

CONTENTS

vii

INTRODUCTION

I have always been fascinated by fairy tales, particularly when I learnt that my name, Teika, means 'fairy tale' or 'legend' in Latvian. I loved everything about the classical fairy tale books I knew as a child: the intriguing titles of the stories, the short, pacy narrative, the characters and the happy endings... I adored too the beautifully-drawn illustrations that accompanied the stories – the heroines and heroes were nearly always dressed in incredible finery. I had to wonder if clothes so beautiful could exist in real life. No doubt inspired by these books and my love of all things fantastical I set about making my own collection of fairy tale books.

The first book I remember making consisted of a small wodge of thick, shiny pieces of paper that were stapled together and illustrated in felt-tipped pen with pictures of characters from *Star Wars*. (Young as I was, it was clear to me that *Star Wars* was basically a fairy tale set in space. It had a Princess, for goodness sake!) On the reverse of the pages there were images of computers that controlled paper-making machines; my father worked for a company which manufactured these futuristic-looking machines, and the paper must have been advertising material. On each page I'd drawn a character accompanied by a few wobbly-looking words. I even threw in the odd joke. I must have been about five or six years old at the time.

Fast forward thirty-three years... I still had this passion to produce a marvellously fantastical book. Thankfully, other writers shared my passion for the fantastical too, so my call for submissions for the first ever fairy tale collection to be published by Mother's Milk Books was met with great enthusiasm!

I was, as ever, humbled by the quality of the submissions. What I love about this collection of stories is the depth and range of writing on show. I feel that these diverse voices, each with their own unique style, complement each other beautifully, giving the reader an insight into the storyteller's psyche. For it is in the nature of fairytales to connect with their audience on an emotional level. There are some powerful connections to be made here.

What I love, too, about this collection is the fact that there are no passive princesses here. Strong women, *real* women, are a feature of the book and although there may not always be a happy ending for them, we can at least give witness to their trials and learn from their tribulations.

I really enjoyed putting together this collection, so much so that my intention is to publish a series of these 'modern fables and ancient tales'.

We are all in need of a little magic these days, and I sincerely hope that this book will provide some escapism; a flight, if you will, into the world of... the forgotten and the fantastical.

Teika Bellamy, Spring 2015

The Boy and the Bird

by NJ Ramsden

The Boy and the Bird

When the world was made it was a dark place and the only light was the light from the sun. But the sun was small in the sky and could only cast its golden arms over one place at a time. It would travel over the face of the earth and while somewhere was hot and bright, anotherwhere was cold and black.

At no particular place in the world there was a forest, and in the forest was a wooded hill. Upon the very top of the hill there stood a humble house, and in the house there lived a boy. During the day the boy would walk in the woods and gather fruits and nuts and listen to the birds sing to one another about things of which only the birds knew. After a good long stroll the boy would return home, stopping off at the well at the bottom of the hill for a well-earned drink. Indoors when it became dark, the boy would huddle up to himself and shiver away through the chilly night.

The boy walked every day and rarely strayed from the paths between the thick tall trees. He knew that if darkness came into the sky while he was very far from home he would become hopelessly lost as he would not be able to see his way. The thought of being alone in the silent shadows without even the birds to guide him, as they sang only in the light of the sun, terrified the boy. So he was careful not to go too far.

At no time in particular, the winds had been playing up. They came from all four corners of the sky and loved to bluster about with whatever they could find. Sometimes it was leaves, which the winds would whip from the trees and toss about in the air. Sometimes it was the boy, and he would struggle to walk as the winds pushed him one way, then another, then another, usually in the wrong direction. He could hear them laugh as they toyed with their fancies, only to become bored and drop them before quietening down and moving on. The winds were bullies, he thought, but they were not always bad, and often just drifted by, passing time, much as did the boy.

On this unparticular occasion, when the boy was out wandering quietly in the forest, enjoying the warmth of the sun on his skin, the light began to flicker – it was there, it was not, it was there and it was not – and a whistling blew his hair, and a coldness filled his bones. It was the winds again. The boy squinted up into the air, and through the branches whisking themselves into a panic he could see a far-off speck being made to dance. As the boy stood curious, the speck grew and its dance became wilder. He watched as the speck became an 'X' whirling in the sky, a letter that was larger by the moment and whose jig was ever more erratic. Then the X began to flap and it was close enough for the boy to see it was a bird.

The wind of the north had been minding its business when it had run into the creature, and begun to play with it, and then the other winds had come along to join in their rough fun. They were torturing the poor thing, thought the boy, when suddenly the bird plunged downwards into the trees. There was a quick flurry of leaves. The winds stopped. The boy's hair settled upon his head, the trees became upright and still, and the sun again shone over the path.

The boy stared into the trees. It was dark under their cover, where the ground sounded hollow and echoes did not dare to go. But he wanted to see if the bird was in need of help and so tentatively he stepped off the path.

'Hello,' he cried. 'Are you there?'

He did not know how far away the bird was, or if it had heard him, so he stepped a little further into the trees.

'Hello!' he cried again. 'Hello!'

Onwards he went, slowly at first and then more quickly, yelling out. Suddenly there was a squawk. 'Wah!' said the bird.

'Here I am!' And the sound came from not too far ahead. The boy ran on, not daring to think of what might be behind him or watching from somewhere invisible. But he came across the bird, which was sitting quite uncomfortably, it seemed, beneath a tree. It was surrounded by broken twigs, and rubbing its wings.

'Who are you?' asked the bird.

'I'm the boy,' said the boy.

'Are you all right?'

'I am a little sore,' said the bird. 'But it's nothing a rest won't cure.'

'You can come to my house if you like,' said the boy. 'I'll feed you and you can stay 'til your wings are better.'

'Thank you,' said the bird. 'I will.'

'It may take some time to find,' said the boy. 'I fear I'm lost away from the path, and it will be dark soon enough, and that worries me.'

'Don't be worried,' said the bird. 'We birds know precisely where we're going.' It tapped its head. 'Magnetic, you know.'

'Goodness,' said the boy. 'That's clever.' He did not know what a magnetic might be, but wished not to appear ignorant.

'Shall we go?'

So the bird stood clumsily up, stretched its legs, and off they went.

No particular time later, the boy and the bird were safely home. The bird was tucked up in bed with bruised wings, and the boy had gathered plenty of things to eat for both of them.

They talked a little, about how the winds were irrepressible bullies, and about how the bird blamed itself for its downfall. 'I curse the winds always,' said the bird, 'because they make flight strenuous. But I shouldn't, because they can also be a great help and lift me when I am tired.'

'It's easy,' said the boy, 'to forget when things are hard that

15

they are not always so.'

The bird agreed. 'I think I may have done it this time though,' it groaned. 'Be glad you couldn't hear me when I came crashing.'

The boy was quiet for no particular length of time, and then said to the bird, 'Would you like a drink? You must be thirsty.'

'I would,' said the bird, so the boy fetched down a beautiful glass he'd once found, and went to the door.

'Where are you going?' asked the bird.

'To the well,' replied the boy, 'to fetch your drink.'

'I'll come with you,' said the bird, 'because you're afraid of the dark and it's become quite dark now, and cold.'

So the bird and the boy walked down the hill to the well. As the boy was leaning over to fill the glass there was a rumble in the sky and a shaking of the ground. The water began to ripple and splash and the boy dropped the glass and it smashed into a thousand pieces. Voices like whispers flew around in the air.

'Bird,' they said as they swished by, 'you've done it this time. You've cursed us once too often and once too strongly.'

It was the winds. They began to blow harder.

'Sorry,' said the bird, a little nervously.

'Yes,' said the boy, a little nervously too.

Swoosh, went the voices. 'Too late for that now,' they said, and blew very hard indeed.

The boy was lifted from his feet and hung in the air for a very short moment before dropping into the well. Splash, he went, and vanished beneath the surface.

The winds laughed. The bird was furious. It rose in the air against the buffeting of the winds and dived into the black water. Down it swam, down into the icy darkness until it came to the bottom where the boy lay in a heap. The bird grabbed the boy and turned back to the surface. Upwards they went, the bird struggling as it was not used to water at all. Upwards they went, and when they burst from the well the boy and the bird were soaked thoroughly through.

'Are you all right?' said the bird and began to flap at the boy to wake him. The boy's eyes opened and the bird said, 'Let's get up that hill into your house.' But the boy was very weak and could not move very fast. When they were halfway up the hill there was a rumbling in the sky and a shaking of the ground and voices like whispers came flying through the air.

'Having fun?' they said. 'We are!' and they blew so hard that the bird was picked up and flung off the side of the hill into the night sky. The boy clung to the bird's back as they tumbled over in the blackness, and the boy screamed and the bird squawked, and round and round they went at the mercy of the winds until the winds became a little tired.

'We must try and escape,' said the bird. 'Hold on.' And they flew upwards.

'I'm cold,' said the boy.

'Take some of my feathers,' said the bird, so the boy plucked some feathers from the breast of the bird and wrapped them around him as a coat. The bird was wet and shivering but flew on upwards with the boy on its back.

The winds started to chase the bird up into the air. The bird went higher and higher, and the air was colder and colder, and the winds followed right behind, upwards and upwards.

Even with his coat of feathers, the boy felt a perishing chill. The bird was flapping slower and slower now, shaking and dripping, its wings painful and its lungs breathless. Higher and higher, up they went – and all of a sudden, stopped.

The bird with the boy on its back hung in the air like a pendant, higher than even the winds could go. They had given up and were watching from far below.

The bird could no longer move. Its wings were so sore and

tired that it just hung in the freezing sky. It was shaking with cold, and the winds looked on as the bird became stiller and stiller and stiller, and they looked on again as frost began to crust over the bird and the boy, and heard it crackle as the frost became ice. The bird saw the boy becoming a glassy ornament and with a burst of strength pecked at the ice until it shattered into a thousand pieces, which exploded all across the night in every direction.

The boy, free of his prison, fell.

He saw the bird finally succumb to the frozen well-water, a ball of shining whiteness in the sky. All around were a thousand tiny twinkling shards. Light seemed to spill from them and brightness shone down. The boy did not remember anything else.

No particular time later, he awoke to the sound of a gentle breeze. He found himself bathing in the sun on the side of the hill on a cushion of leaves. The winds must have put me here, thought the boy. They must have dried him off too, along with the sun, because he was no longer cold and shivering and wet. He felt his coat of feathers and thought of the bird which seemed like a dream to him now. But when the sun had passed over, and night came after all, the boy looked out of his window and saw a sky full of shining lights. He went outside in his warming coat, and stared up at them. They were beautiful, a spangled blanket – and over all, one great white bloom, a nightlight that glowed down across the paths and tickled the treetops, a glow like ice that was not ice, white and welcoming.

The dark was not so dark as it had been. And as the boy walked down the hill and through the forest, the light followed him wherever he went. The winds did not bother him again, and was the boy ever a bit chilly in the night, he would wrap himself in the feather coat and stand outside on the hill.

He would hold out his arms and wish to be a bird.

Screaming Sue

by Marija Smits

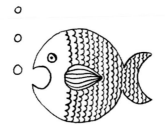

Screaming Sue

'So you wanna know the real story? Off the record? Yeah sure, why not? I can't see your goody-two-shoes editor wanting to print my ghoulish tale anyway. Wouldn't look too good alongside the photos of me in my tux next to my radiant bride-to-be. Besides, you'd never believe me.

'So where should I start? Hang on a minute. Sure you don't want a drink? No? Too bad, this is a damn fine scotch.

'So... you probably already know most of my life story: distant relative of the Kennedys, father in politics, mother a scientist. Been through Harvard law school, top of the class. Forever in the papers — us rich kids always are. Parties, booze, girlfriends, scandals... God it's all so tedious.

'What's that, drugs? Seriously? You gotta be kidding. My mom's a goddamn chemist. I know about the shit they cut stuff with.

'Okay, okay... I've dabbled, but I like to be in control of my own mind, thank you very much. Ha! I'm a goddamn control freak if you wanna know the truth.'

'Anyway. So I've just finished college; Pops wants me to go into politics and Mom tells me I should follow my own path. I kinda like her idea. She says, "Take some time out, discover what you're passionate about. Experience the world." But in private, Dad's all like, "Son, you got a responsibility to this family. We expect great things from you. Sure, take a year out, mess about, but if you're not serious about anything or anyone by the end of the year, you better damn well get married to someone of my choosing and start working for me. I don't want an unemployed bum for a son — and I don't want you out boozing, dragging our good family name through the mud and being linked to every goddamn young woman prepared to get her tits and ass out for the camera. Got it?"

'Sure I get it. Dad'll cut me out of my inheritance if I don't do as he wants, and if there's one thing us rich kids don't like, it's this: hard work.

'So I take a year out. Throw a lot of parties on my yacht. Have one fling after the other. But it kinda sucks... because it's like this race against time. One year to find what I'm passionate about. One year to find a woman I love enough to want to marry. That's one huge goddamn time bomb waiting to go off.

'And as the months go by I get kinda frantic, you know, throwing more and more parties, hooking up with even more women... boozing heavily. I just want to blot the whole year out. It's only when I'm alone on the yacht, fishing, that I feel some kind of peaceful.

'Then one day I decide I've had enough. I sail north, away from the temptations of the harbours and cities, into real quiet territory, and all I do is fish. I don't catch much, so when I see a small trawler I ask the fishermen what's up with all the fish, or rather, lack of fish. They look at me like I'm a madman, and ask me what planet I've been living on for the last couple of years. Don't I know that these waters have been overfished and that there's hardly anything left? They tell me that they only just about make a living by trawling the seabed for all the ugly-looking critters that live down there. I ask them if there's any waters round here where the catch may be better. No, they say, otherwise they'd be there like a shot. Then this one old guy directs me further north. He says that if I'm man enough I could try Coos Bay. So what's in Coos Bay? I say. A real rocky coastline, the old man says. And the ghost, screaming Sue.

'So I gotta ask: Who the hell is screaming Sue? So the old guy tells me that she's some dame who disobeyed her father a real long time ago. Nobody knows what the hell her old daddy didn't approve of, 'cause it happened so long ago, but to cut a long story short, her daddy's having none of it. He drags her out into the bay and drowns her. The place has been haunted ever since. And the fishermen don't ever go near it.

'So as you can imagine, I'm well and truly hooked. I've simply got to find this Sue, maybe catch a whole load of fish too, so I give my thanks to the fishermen and sail further north.

'The coast is one helluva mass of jagged rocks, and even though it's getting late I drop anchor and take my rowing boat out. I'm damn well gonna get amongst those rocks, catch what I can catch, and maybe give that spook a run for its money.

'And the weird thing is... it's just so damn peaceful. The setting sun is making all these barnacle-covered rocks glow golden, the waters are sparkling, and I'm catching all kinds of fish. And I have a memory of my dad and me, fishing, on our yacht, at sunset. I must've been about ten years old at the time. Pop's eating cherries, spitting the stones out into the water, and he's got this peaceful look about him, like he's the king of the world, or something. And it's then that I realize what I want to do. I want to goddamn fish, and I want there to be enough fish in these waters to do that. Re-populating the waters ain't rocket science. It's about the law, money, and politics. And I can sure as hell manage all three of them.

'So I'm sitting and thinking, all excited-like, when I see something in the bay that nearly makes me shit my pants. It looks just like the head of a person, bobbing up and down in the water; hair floating around it. I row over to it because even though I'm as scared as hell, I just gotta take a look. And when I get close I realize it's just a seaweed-covered buoy. I nearly piss myself laughing, I'm that relieved. So I give the buoy a good hard thump, 'cause I can, and then the *real* weird shit starts to happen.

'I can hear something stirring in the water, close to the buoy. Suddenly the "something" bursts out of the water, and the air is filled with the sound of screaming. And this thing is screaming, and thrashing and flailing about, just like a person who's drowning. Only it's not a person. It's a skeleton.

'I'm telling you, I was scared all right. So I row as fast as I can back to the yacht. I'm nearly there when I take one last look at the skeleton. And the damnedest thing happens. I suddenly realize that this "thing" was once a person. A real, flesh and blood person. And this soul, person, woman — whatever — is in pain.

'Part of me just wants to get the hell out of there, but another part of me wants to stay and help. Maybe it's a guy thing — I don't know — but I turn the boat around and go back. And although it's getting dark, I can see that the skeleton must be somehow tethered to the seabed, so I dive into the water and my arm comes into contact with a chain. I catch hold of the chain and pull. It must be attached to an anchor, or something, because it's as heavy as hell and I really don't think I'm gonna be able to haul it up when something gives, or breaks... and the thrashing stops.

'So I surface, desperate for air, and realize that I musta somehow got the skeleton free, 'cause the screaming's stopped and it's just floating away, all peaceful-like.

'But then the really nasty-looking shit begins to happen. Fish – like thousands of them – are coming out of nowhere and swimming towards the skeleton. They're brushing past me and freaking me out so I get back in the boat, real quick. It's as if they're swarming round the corpse, ready to carry it off. So I'm guessing that they're gonna pick apart all those bones, and I suddenly feel real sad. But they don't. Instead, they're kinda puking on the skeleton. It's totally disgusting and I really don't wanna watch but I do 'cause it's fascinating in a horrific kind of way. Then suddenly they stop their regurgitating – or whatever – and swim away. And what they've left behind is a woman. Naked, and beautiful as hell.

'So I row over to her and drag her outta the water and into my boat. I check for a pulse and find one.

'And for once, I don't know what the hell to do — whether to try to resuscitate her or not. 'Cause she's breathing all right, and her pulse is strong, but she's completely out for the count. So I don't bother with the resuscitation. I'm guessing that she needs to go to hospital, so I row back to the yacht, bring her aboard and put her on the sofa in the lounge. I down a couple of glasses of scotch and try to think what to do — either call for the coastguard or sail to the nearest port and get some medical assistance there. And then I realize what I'll look like, asking for help for an unconscious, naked woman I've just found in the water, who happens to have been regurgitated back to life by a whole bunch of fish. And I think about my dad, and what *he'll* say when he hears what's happened.

'"What the *hell* am I thinking?" I say to myself. So I sit on the floor, with my back against the sofa and I keep ahold of her hand. I knock back another bottle of scotch while I recite a silent prayer: Wake up. For God's sake, for my sake, wake up.

'Then I pass out.'

'Next thing I know is that I'm awake and daylight is streaming through the windows. I turn to look at the sofa but the woman's no longer there. I get up as quickly as my spinning head will let me and I go out on deck. And there she is, in one of my white T-shirts and a pair of black shorts, just standing against the guardrail, looking out to sea.

'She then turns to face me. "Well," she says, looking at me like I'm an idiot. "And what do you want?"

'"Me," I says, my heart beating like a goddamn drum, "I don't want anything."

'So she looks back at the ocean, her wild black hair streaming out behind her.

'My heart's still beating like a drum gone crazy and I have to tell myself to get a grip. "Who are you?" I say to her. "And what the hell happened last night?"

'She turns to look at me. "I'm Susanna," she says, "and last night the fish returned to me what they took all those decades ago."

'She stares at me, real hard, and then says, "And I suppose you want me to thank you?"

'"No," I say, shaking my head.

'"Well, what *do* you want?" she asks.

'"Nothin', really," I say. "I mean, I want a couple of things – like for there to be more fish in these waters. And," I say, a grin on my face, "a good woman would be a bonus."

'But she just laughs at me and then turns back to look at the sea. "I could help you get the fish back," she says, "that's easy enough." She looks at me again. "But making them stay — that's the hard part. Would you be up to the challenge?"

'"Yeah, sure," I say, but then I'm distracted by the fact that she's climbing over the guardrail. "And what the hell do you think you're doing now?" I ask.

'"I've got things to do," she says. "Old bones that I need to make peace with."

'And then she dives off the boat.

'"But will I ever see you again?" I shout after her.

'She looks at me one last time. "Maybe."

'And then she's gone, her crazy black curls sinking under the waves.'

'Days pass. Weeks. And all I do is wait. And fish, and think, while my heart slowly breaks.

'One night I go to bed thinking that I can't take anymore of this so I get up and pour myself a drink or two...

'I wake up on the sofa in the lounge the next morning, my head hammering away. I go out on deck to get some fresh air, and there's Sue again, lying on a sunlounger. Naked, and beautiful as hell. Her wet T-shirt and shorts are on the seat beside her, getting dry in the sun. She opens her eyes and then smiles at me...

***

'And? And what? What the hell kinda question is that? I'm sure you can figure out what happened next. And not long after that, we got engaged to be married.

'Yeah, me and Susanna have got this big fancy wedding coming up. Not our thing really, but we're happy enough to play along with my parents' wishes. That's why we're okay about having our pictures in your glossy magazine. But as soon as the wedding's over, we're sailing away for a couple of weeks.

'Never you mind where we're sailing to. That's none of your goddamn business. Anyway, what about you? I can tell you've got your own personal time bomb ticking away.

'How long have you been with your boyfriend for? Two months? And does your heart beat like a drum gone crazy when you're with him? No? Then do yourself and him a favour and break it off. The relationship's dead already. Honour its passing, feel what you gotta feel and then move on.

'What is it that you want to do? Not this hack work, I take it? You wanna write? A novel, yeah? Then write it. Just get on and write it.

'Me? Yeah, I've got big plans too. I'm gonna damn well increase the stocks of fish on the West Coast. Then me and Sue are gonna sail away into the sunset.

'And no goddamn time bomb is *ever* gonna get us.'

Footfalls of the Hunter

by Lindsey Watkins

Footfalls of the Hunter

The soft touch of skin on skin, downy hair on downy hair, and the equal pressure of soft girl lips on soft girl lips. *Come, get into bed with me.*

Hunter hung up her tunic and wrestled her face and arms into her jumper. Taking her satchel from under a chair, she clattered down the steep, rickety steps of the surgery to the kennels where a large mongrel with yellow eyes glared at her accusingly. A low growl, hauntingly familiar. Hunter felt a jolt somewhere inside her chest. Disquieted, she glanced again at the dog and wondered, wasn't it you I left to rot on the sweet earthy ground? No, of course not, no, that was another. The dog whined faintly and lay down, resting head on paws, eyes softened and doleful.

Hunter let herself out at the front of the practice and set off along the lane, scuffling through the soggy autumnal sludge at the side of the road, under canopy of oak and beech and birch. Dusk. Seven o'clock and already pitchy: dark as a ditch in the trees. But on the road, where the moonlight reflected off the shiny pot-hole puddles, Hunter could see her path well.

It was just here actually, just where the path opens into the forest between the two birch trees, that it had happened. But when? An age ago.

Hunter stopped and stroked the twinkling glister of a silver birch; she shuddered at the memory of two arylide yellow eyes, floating on the black night. How had she known those eyes had been waiting for her? How had she known that night to pack her satchel with a needle, a knife and a blanket? How had she known to enter the forest that night? Some errant call...

But no time for dallying by the birches now... only time for hurrying home to the tender kisses of the find, the fruit of that full-moon night. Hunter set off again with a quickened pace. The forest was left behind and in the village a door opened, arms and mouths opened and met and fitted.

Next day, early, around the time stirring starts. A hint of light was breathing through the curtains, revealing a soft burrow of cotton and down. Two girls, sheet-wrapped and sleeping. Two bodies warm, sleep-softened and entangled like ivy: leg with leg with arm and breast.

The warm softness was hiding a nightmare inside. Scarlet was dreaming and all was noise and dark terror: the thud, thud, thud of wolf heart, strong and male and lusting. And slime and slurry against the naked body; the burn of bubbling acid on tender skin. And the knowledge of being lost in a consuming blend of nature's ancient chemicals. Rhythmic thuds: wolf heart, wolf heart, wolf heart... or something else? Could it be steady thudding footfalls on the mossy earth bed? Footfalls of the hunter?

Scarlet woke with a start, eyes wide with the horror of memory. And then, senses engaged, she felt again the soft touch of Hunter's flesh, and the safety of it. Their bodies tangled in a puzzle of likeness. Four legs wrapped together in comfortable knowledge. Hip pressed to hip, alike and yet not, as if from the same sibling mould. On the threshold of otherness; on the threshold of identity.

'Hun, you awake?'

'Mmm, nearly.'

'Tell me again, Hun, tell me how you did it.'

'I'll dream it, and you can listen,' said Hunter, sleepily. 'I'll hold you tight at the scary bits.' And she went back there again...

Back between the birch trees on that full moon night. Hunter's steady thudding footfalls on the mossy earth bed; her agile body ducking under ash branch, vaulting beech root and dodging the woody columns of a nameless pre-Doric order. Hunter's satchel slapped rhythmically on her thigh: bump of needle, blade and towel. The ancient wood, dark and ominous, the oldest of feudal friends, urged her on with its barky creaks; the silent ringing of a thousand bluebells tinkled and clattered their bidding.

In a moonlit clearing, where beady bull's eye windows of a cottage glared at her, she stopped. The echo of the last footfall faded and Hunter's ears retuned in the quiet to register the rustle of a distant wind-caught leaf and the faint hoot of an owl. She hooked the satchel over her head and crouched with it near the ground, feeling inside for her tools, all the while her eyes and ears alert with expectancy.

Then, chin to knee, Hunter waited and watched.

And then from behind the dumpy stone cottage came two arylide yellow eyes, floating on the black night. A sniff of curiosity, of suspicion and the eyes advanced, becoming figure, becoming animal, becoming wolf.

Not five yards from Hunter, the beast let out a low snarling growl of curiosity. Hunter's nerves were electrified and she suddenly knew why the needle, why the blade, why the towel.

Taking off first her T-shirt and then her trousers and underwear, she let him see her nakedness. The clothes were discarded on the ground; they would no longer be needed. The pale flesh and the lust which was gathering in her body at once tamed him and untamed him. The wolf hungered but he failed to realise how Hunter's own hunger delved into and then somehow beyond him.

Closer now, her face nuzzled his bristly scruff, his spiky cheeks, his stubbly snout, while her hand brushed over the wiry hackles. Wolf's eyes closed as he allowed desire to surge up from his horny claws through the mass of muscle. In that

33

moment of greedy anticipation, did the beast even notice the sharp scratch and then the force which sent the sedative seeping through muscle to the bloodstream?

He noticed it and he knew. No tamed mutt now; gnashing and gnarling in the fury of capture, the unjustness and confusion of an outsmarting. Yellow eyes narrowed in anger. Muscle and claw swiped and clawed. But Hunter sprang out of reach, patiently, nakedly, and the claws clutched only heavy forest air.

Then terrific thump of bulk, and a silence.

Hunter heaved the collapsed hulk of drug-tamed animal so that the belly lay upmost. From her satchel she drew the blade. With her left hand she parted the straggling matt of gut covering. And then firm and precise, she made the first incision: umbilicus to pubis – a moonlit symmetry of half wolf and half wolf. Then second incision, through the shiny jelly thickness of subcutaneous fat; a third incision through the rich bloody muscles of abdominal wall. Then a deep lust-coloured cavern. Hunter delved elbow deep, around slopping organs, her fingers probing for her prize. Finding the lumpy misshapen stomach, she eased it gently but firmly to the incision. Another cut, and then a gentle easing as a slippery sloppy tangle of limbs and hips and breasts slipped out on to the earth.

Gently and urgently, with the towel, Hunter wiped the slime from the body in front of her: from the fingertips, from the hands and wrists, the arms, and then the toes and feet and ankles, knees and thighs, crotch and stomach and buttocks and back, from the breasts and the chest and the shoulder blades and the neck, from the cheeks and the eyelids and the dark red lips. The wiping touch warmed and wakened the body. Eyes opened and widened and were hazel, and skin was rosy, and hair was ebony and nothing was scarlet, except that this was Scarlet and Hunter had found her and saved her.

A wolf corpse lay, still and gaping, and ready to rot on the sweet earthy ground. So captivated with Scarlet was Hunter, that she did not take the time to fill the belly with stones and sew it up again; so snug was Scarlet wrapped in the arms of Hunter, that she did not think to skin the devil and fashion a coat.

The soft touch of skin on skin, downy hair on downy hair, and the equal pressure of soft girl lips on soft girl lips. *Come, get into bed with me.*

The Mother Tree

by CM Little

The Mother Tree

Since time began, stories have grown from our earth. They are given life by the rich soil of the land and the pathways of tales are overgrown with its produce.

Apples, of course, are distant cousins of legend and fairytale. The golden apples given to Zeus and Hera as a wedding gift, guarded by the Hesperides and stolen by Eris, to become an instrument of discord are merely the start of the storytelling fruit.

Apples hold the truth within these stories: the red apple given to Snow White that was laced with poison gave its warning through the brash colour of its skin; at the beginning of time, Eve and then Adam were tempted with the taste of an apple and its promise of knowledge absolute.

The branches that bear fruit are laden too with words passed down through generations. They have protected: briars shielding a sleeping beauty or a laurel tree taking on Daphne's spirit to protect her from an unwelcome god. They have also played a more sinister role: losing the hapless Hansel and Gretel in their collective darkness, hiding a wolf seeking its Red Riding Hood. And yet more, they have sheltered and inspired and enlightened: the spreading arms of the Banyan tree have provided riches more than gold to those who meditate in their shade.

For some, it is a tree that represents life itself: Yggdrasil, the tree that brings together the heavens, hells and all in between. You may know of the ympe-tre then, and of how the Faerie King came through the grafted branches in a dream to Heurodis and stole her away. Only the sweetest music of Orfeo could win her back again.

Lesser known is the tale of the Mother Tree, which brought forth nourishment such as you've never dreamed. Let me tell you the tale.

There was once an old gardener who worked in the orchards outside the palace. He had been apprenticed to the head gardener as a young boy and remained all his life learning his trade and tending to the trees. He never married and so he loved the plants as his own children. He nurtured seedlings to mature trees and rejoiced each year in the fruit that they produced. There were apple trees with varieties that ranged so far that they were a world in themselves. Golden Delicious, the golden yellow apple that tasted of sunshine and honey, Egremont Russet with its rough skin that belied the soft, yielding interior. Granny Smith, a bold green apple, crisp and fresh with a body that demanded your teeth to do their work. Pink Lady, the blushing aristocrat of the orchard whose pastel-coloured skin belied the bitter bite within. And the gardener's favourite, Gala, the common red and green, run-of-the-mill apple that you may buy in any market or shop worth its apples. But the taste, the gardener always said, was anything but common.

'Tell me where else you may find sweetness and freshness combined so perfectly,' he would challenge any non-believers. Handing them a sample from the orchard, he would find his challenge successful.

It was hard work to tend an orchard and the gardener showed it in the lines on his weather-beaten face and the calluses on his hands. Most recently, he had started to create a family tree. This is an old magic by which three or four (for the adventurous) varieties of apple are grafted onto a single tree. Rather than being burdened by the new fruit, the tree seems to grow in strength from what is grafted on to it.

It is, of course, known as a family tree as it supports a number of varieties of the apple family. And although grafting may be seen by weathered gardeners as day-to-day normality and simply the appliance of a bit of science, this particular gardener, and I agree with him, never failed to see a little bit of magic in this.

One day, the king summoned the gardener to meet with him. The gardener spent much of the morning cleaning the ingrained dirt of garden work from his hands and tugging at his hair, trying to make it lie flat in such a way as it would look obedient to the king. The gardener, free of his duties, stood nervously in the grand hallway of the palace waiting to be received. Much of his time was spent worrying at his cap.

The king, who was plucked straight from every childhood fairytale you have ever read, was kindly but secure in his authority and made the gardener wait just a few minutes longer than was necessary. He sat atop his throne, which was slightly raised on a platform, and nodded as the gardener gave an awkward bow.

'I wish to discuss the apple harvest and the celebrations we will give.' By "we", the king of course meant himself. The gardener had never understood why members of the royal family multiplied in such a way, but he wisely kept his own counsel and remained quiet, waiting for an invitation to speak.

'We shall have a grand party, starting with a tour of the orchard in which guests may pick apples themselves.' By this, the gardener understood that guests may point to an apple so that a mere servant could then pluck the apple, wash it and then hand it to them.

'We shall have a feast that evening and apples will be the theme,' said the king, by which the gardener understood he must speak with the cook and arrange between them a suitably grand banquet.

The king leant forward and he whispered, 'And we shall give to our queen a present. A tree shall be placed at the end of the orchard and from this tree she shall pluck her favourite apple.' He sat back and nodded, indicating that the discussion was over.

Uncertain of himself, the gardener cleared his throat and, when the king indicated he might speak, asked, 'Would you tell me please the variety of apple that the queen favours?'

The king said with a frown, 'Details? You want details? I have told you what I want. Now go away and make it happen.' And after a pause, sternly, 'On pain of all you hold dear, make it so.'

Unfair, thought the gardener, leaving the room still facing the king, but he realized he could ask the queen's staff and favourites within the court for her preferred apple type.

Harder than I'd thought, realized the gardener, when halfway through a discussion with the kitchen staff.

'She enjoyed that crumble that time,' mused one cook.

'The rhubarb crumble you mean! Yes, very helpful,' retorted another.

'It's those little yellow ones I've seen her eat most often.'

'Ananas Reinette?' asked the gardener hopefully.

'Yellow apples?' said a passing maid, quite happy to interrupt. 'No, no, the queen will only eat the crisp green ones!'

'Oh no,' said the butler, 'you will find that her lady has a particular love of soft red apples — the precise name escapes me'.

As the staff crowding the room descended into bickering, the gardener shook his head and went to speak with the queen's own ladies-in-waiting.

A little haughtily, the ladies agreed to speak with the gardener, although they kept their distance lest the dirt from the garden muddy their expensive gowns and jewels.

'Her ladyship's preferred apple?' they exclaimed, every syllable deliberately and carefully pronounced. They looked at each other for some time before the youngest and least haughty replied, 'Her ladyship does not, to my knowledge, like apples. She prefers carefully crafted pastries and sculpted cakes. Apples are a little...' her voice faltered.

'Rustic?' suggested the lady beside her.

The gardener was more than a little nervous around the fine ladies. He wasn't altogether sure what they meant by "rustic" and why it would prevent the queen from enjoying a tasty fruit. As he left the room, he merely worried how he could provide a favourite apple for a queen who did not like or approve of apples.

The worry remained with him as he wandered through the orchard later that same day. By then, the sun was beginning to lower in the sky and the colours were reflected on the trees, bathing them in half-light, a red tinge finally turning to dark. As night set its calm over the orchard, the gardener's natural smile returned. He knew what to do.

The next few months were hard work, harder than usual, but in the approach to the apple harvest, the gardener felt proud of his orchard and, when summoned to explain himself in front of the king, spoke humbly but with pride of his apples. He had confidence that the cook had in hand a menu of refinement and taste that would present the fruit in all its nuanced flavours.

'And my final order,' the king stated, rather than asked.

The gardener smiled in the most humble way he could and nodded.

'The queen's favourite apple will be ready for her to pluck from a tree,' he stated simply.

The king expected nothing else and gestured that the gardener was dismissed.

As the summer drew to an end and the autumn days grew shorter, the gardener put the finishing touches to the fine display that would greet the guests. When the day of the celebration dawned, he rose before the sun and awaited its lazy greeting with a tapping foot of impatience. There were many last minute touches that could not have been done before the day itself and the gardener found himself in charge of an outdoor household staff, down to the placing of the ladies-in-waiting around the orchard. Rustic, the word echoed in his ears, as he steered the elbow of the young lady who had given him the worrying news.

'Rustic may be coarse and unrefined,' he said quietly but firmly, as he placed her by a tree, 'but it may also have its charms and hold its own magic.' He smiled at her surprise and left her to wonder.

Mid-afternoon, the guests started to arrive in all their finery. *They* certainly seemed to see the charm in a rustic setting and there were gasps of surprise and laughs of delight as they approached to see the baskets filled with apples, colours so vivid they could only be artifice, surely? But beyond the baskets overflowing with fruit, the fine lords and ladies came to an avenue with a carpet of lush green grass, lined either side with trees still laden with apples.

The trees formed walls that began a deep red, the Arkansas Black and Autumn Gold forming a bright pattern with the green leaves. This gave way through the mixed Early Windsor to a yellow section, Ginger Gold and Pitmaston Pineapple leading the guests on.

All the while, they were encouraged by bejewelled ladies-in-waiting to have what fruit they would from the trees and to savour the taste. The enjoyment of the colours soon gave way to refined nibbling and appreciative murmurs. Finally, a pure green section of tree wall greeted the party, the crisp Granny Smiths and the bitter Bramleys perfectly complementing one another, with partner pear trees, one across the way from the other, providing a final sweetness, the fine Williams pears resting in the mouths of the guests for as long as they lasted, the perfect dessert to a feast of apples.

And at the end of the avenue stood a lone tree, but not one like the others – this tree had a small circle of deep purple flowers around its base and each of the apples that adorned it had a tiny white crown around its stalk.

The king bowed to the queen as they drew away from the crowd and he pointed at the tree, 'Your favourite apple, grown especially for you.'

As he spoke, the sun, which had been high in the sky, began to fall and, as it did, light fell upon the tree and illuminated all its fruit. There were no gasps; the people were silent as one apple glinted gold and another shone bright red, another glowed deep green. Every one of the apples was a slightly different colour.

The queen broke the silence with a laugh that rang of delighted surprise. 'One tree with one, two, three – how many different apples?'

She approached the tree alone and held the golden apple in her hand, Golden Delicious, she read from the label that crowned the fruit. And Cox's Orange Pippin from another. Quizzically, more like a young girl than a queen, she turned to the king and then to the gardener. Her head shook slightly and her hands spread out in the universal gesture of question.

Glancing first at the king for permission, the gardener spoke softly. 'Your Majesty, for you this is no ordinary apple tree. This is the finest artistry that ever has adorned a tree. For no fewer than forty different varieties of apple grow on this one tree. I have named it, if you would agree, the Mother Tree.'

'The Mother Tree,' said the queen, nodding in agreement.

As the sun's light faded, she stopped and picked from the tree a modest, brown apple. A russet.

'My favourite.'

She smiled, then bit into the flesh, a little of the sweet juice running onto her chin.

Grief Trilogy

by Becky Cherriman

Grief

Lest they forget, they named their second baby Grief. She fought her way out, tearing at her father's guts as she wrenched herself from her mother's womb into the turmoil of day.

The other babies they knew smiled at four weeks and chuckled at ten. Not Grief. Thin as parchment and cold as coins over a dead man's eyelids, she simply stared vacantly up at them. Nor did she cry, or at least not aloud. Her tears were on the inside, tightly woven into the sinews of her forget-me-not heart.

For though even the midwife couldn't bear to touch her and her presence scarred the memories of anyone who met her, her parents bore her close. When the weight became too much, they passed her to the other. Then feeling guilty at her absence snatched her back.

And Grief, she grew.

Manqué

John's breath was rattling in his lungs when she came.

He mistook her for Death at first; it was her blotched flesh, the stench of decomposing vegetation. He hadn't yet realised that for him Death would have the texture of fresh earth, the scent of bluebells.

Grief hovered for a while on the landing, savouring the vacant in-betweeness of it.

Then she entered and placed her fingers on his sweat-soaked forehead.

The memories rippled in — an eddy of electric eels — and, on the current, the times his children's 'I love yous' had gone unanswered; the buffeting caress of surf; his pacifist position as a youth and that row with his father before the old man's yomp to war, and his death — the death John had never mourned.

And the last jolt was a word — manqué — that which might have been but is not, that which has missed being.

John lay, convulsing, till Grief removed her hand and he wept; he wept for the first time since a jam-stained seven-year-old had found Duke's mangled paw in the mousetrap.

Then he picked up a pen, began to write. He wrote a letter to his father, to his younger pacifistic self, to the roll of the sea. And when he had finished, he looked up to find that Grief had gone.

In the air was the scent of bluebells.

Grief and the Boy

Grief moved on and found a boy bitter as lemon and steeped in gin. He was standing at the cliff edge, looking over. He did not look surprised to see her.

He told her about a girl he'd met, a girl who laughed like it was always summer. She had loved him with the timbre of her words and her inquisitive mind. She had loved him with slender stroking fingers and with her eyes. She had heard his secrets and stayed.

He had first seen her here, by the ocean, in rolled-up jeans playing a harmonica. The next day she had been guiding a blind woman at the harbour edge. He knew he didn't know her and yet he was compelled by such a sense of knowing her that he had walked over and leaned on the railing next to them as though that simple act was his life's vocation.

'Perhaps it was,' Grief accused.

The boy ignored her and told of how one evening they had been sitting hand-in-hand on the rooftop above the fish-and-chip shop where the girl lived when she had spotted something on the ground below. Investigating, they found a swallow. Its feathers had been pecked half-off, leaving a fetid wound on its face and a broken wing. The boy thought it beyond saving but the girl befriended the trembling creature, wrapped it up in her cardigan and carried it into the warm.

Over the days that followed, the swallow came to trust her, and the boy too. The boy grew fond of the swallow and, for a while, the three of them lived happily together in her flat above the fish-and-chip shop.

Eventually, through the girl's ministrations, the swallow healed. And when it was time they went out together, into the dunes. The couple waited, braced against the elements and one another, shoulders touching, until they sensed the swallow was ready. The girl held out her palm. And the swallow flew.

But though he had regained the freedom of the skies the bird chose to stay because of his love for the girl.

Grief stormed in the sky above the boy. She screamed from the grey swell beneath and she raged in the wind around him. 'So where is she now?' she taunted. 'Where is she now?'

Yet of course Grief knew and the boy hated her for it. But he hated himself more so he yelled into the wind and spat his confessions into the sea. 'I betrayed her, the girl who heard my secrets and stayed. I let another woman love me with her slender stroking fingers but she did not love me with her eyes.' He quietened. 'And when I came back, the girl I loved was gone and our swallow lay lifeless on the asphalt roof.'

Grief made no reply but the boy could see her clearly now. She had swelled from a voice in the wind to a grotesque face that enveloped the whole grey sky, her great mouth opening in a putrid mess of rotting teeth and stale blood.

Some say the boy leapt into the sea, others that he simply moved away. Those of us who know the maw of Grief's hunger hope that they are right.

The Wanderer's Dream

by Barbara Higham

The Wanderer's Dream

Once upon a time there were two women called Tanwen and Vanessa. Both liked telling stories very much. Tanwen's occupied many an evening. She was brimful of ideas for crafting into new adventures and was fond of talking. Vanessa was a quiet poet, who pondered for months at a time over every word of the verse she wrote. Seldom did she recite her poems to anyone. The two women had long been firm friends and each found great pleasure in the other's words.

One summer's day they wandered together through the countryside. They roamed up hill and down dale, until late in the afternoon they sat themselves down in the tickly grass beside a stream, ate their remaining warm flattened sandwiches, and drank cold clear water from the stream that tumbled over the rocks. Vanessa lay back in the grass, stretched her tired limbs, and gazed up into the blue blue blue. Presently, lulled by the lapping of the water on the stones, her eyelids grew heavy and she began to drift off. Meanwhile Tanwen watched the white-bellied sand martins flitting over the water and disappearing into holes in the bank. 'And I felt sure we'd see a kingfisher by the water today,' she said, turning to her friend, but Vanessa was fast asleep so did not reply.

As the two friends rested, the sun sent long shadows across the grass of this fine day approaching evening. Tanwen was looking on the peaceful face of her companion, when a most peculiar thing happened. As the sleeping woman breathed rhythmically, her lips parted and from her open mouth there emerged a white butterfly! It alighted on her shoulder, spreading out its wings, each with two small black spots and grey tipped tops. The insect crept along her arm, then the length of her long leg, fluttered onto the ground, moved through the short grass, and skittered down the bank to the water's edge. Before this petal-winged creature lay a row of stepping-stones of millstone grit, glittering with crystals of glassy quartz and protruding from a shallow part of the stream. The butterfly made its way across the water, pausing for a few moments on each one of these sandy stones.

Mesmerised, Tanwen leapt up and with a skip and a jump followed the butterfly across the water to the far side. Along the stream Indian balsam flowered purple in profusion for the bees' delight. The butterfly flew from one bloom to the next and then off, over the grass, to where lay the skull of an animal. It had certainly lain there some considerable time, as it was quite bare and bleach-weathered. Tanwen thought it too big to have come from a sheep's head and did not know to what creature it might once have belonged. In through the eye socket of the white bone flew the butterfly. Tanwen kept quite still, a little bewildered by what she was seeing. She kept her eyes fixed on the skull, while a nearby sheep looked up from its grazing to glance at the woman before going back to its chewing.

After a while — Tanwen could not tell you for the life of her how long she had really stood there — the butterfly flew out and flitted past her, back to the purple flowers, and then over the stepping-stones, descending from the air and settling upon each one in turn. It crept up the stream's bank and through the grass, making straight for the prone Vanessa. When it reached the sleeping figure it hopped onto her foot, crawled along her leg and up her chest that was gently rising and falling with each restful breath, then jumped onto her chin, and straight into her open mouth.

At once Vanessa shut her mouth and sat up rubbing her eyes. 'I nodded off!' She yawned. 'Have I been asleep for ages?'

'Not long,' replied her friend, puzzling over the disappearance of the butterfly, 'but while you were sleeping I saw *the* most amazing thing!'

Vanessa, usually the more reticent of the two, for once had to speak first, 'I had the most peculiarly vivid dream that I went on a long journey. I must have been away for years! I went wandering for miles and miles though high-grassed meadows, where the grass grew higher than my head, then down to the sea. I was sailing far across an ocean from one island to the next until I reached a distant land, where I passed though forests of... *honey* stretching to the heavens. I was overcome with a sense of wonder at everything I saw: the sights, the smells, the tastes! Suddenly, a vast palace of white marble sprung up before me. I went straight in to this imposing building and lingered about the cool and empty space. There was absolutely nothing there, only the loveliness of the light that bathed me. I was thinking perhaps I might stay there forever, so serene was I, when suddenly an odd feeling came over me and I knew I had to go back at once.

'So off I went, out the way I had come. Back across the tall sweet-flowered forests and across the sea, stopping at many ports along the way. I trudged once again through the tallest grassed fields for many miles, before I reached home. I had just closed my front door and was thinking about supper, when I woke up here! Fancy!'

Tanwen stood quietly for a moment musing over what her friend had told her and then she replied, 'Come with me and I shall show you exactly where you have just been!' And the woman, who was freshly slept-out, jumped to her feet and followed her friend down the bank, listening as Tanwen told the incredible story of how she had seen the white butterfly crawl out of her mouth after she had fallen asleep.

'This,' said Tanwen, 'where we are walking now, is the tallest grass you trekked through. This stream is the vast ocean and those stepping-stones the islands you landed upon. The

Indian balsam on the other side of our stream is the honeyed forest of the distant land and that animal's skull just there the big empty palace you ventured into!'

Both women had indeed seen wonders! But, I ask myself, which of the two had seen the greater?

The Sparrows and the Beefworms: a fable

by Rebecca Burland

The Sparrows and the Beefworms: a fable

Once upon a time, there was a field with trees all around its edges. And these trees were the homes of lots of sparrow families.

Every spring, when the baby sparrows hatched out of their eggs, the mummy sparrows would spend their days rooting around in the field for worms to take back to their babies. The mummies enjoyed hunting, and the babies grew into healthy young sparrows. If one of the mummy sparrows had difficulties in finding worms the other sparrows would help her out.

But then one day a new sparrow arrived in the field. She told the mummy sparrows that she was an expert in baby sparrow nutrition. She watched them flying to and from the field, and she said to them, 'That looks like hard work! You shouldn't feed your babies whenever they seem hungry, you'll wear yourself out. Feed them every few hours, and then you won't have to spend so much time hunting for worms!'

'But we don't mind hunting for worms!' said the mummy sparrows.

'And you'll still be able to do it,' said the expert, 'but this way you'll have more time to tidy the nest and talk to the other sparrows!'

The mummy sparrows weren't sure but, because she was an expert, they did as she said. Every day they anxiously watched the sun move across the sky so they could know when to hunt for worms for their hungry babies.

But then something strange happened – the baby sparrows didn't grow into healthy young sparrows. They were small and thin, and always seemed hungry! The mummy sparrows flew to the expert sparrow asking for advice.

'Ah,' said the expert sparrow. 'You clearly cannot collect enough worms for your babies to thrive. This is quite common, you know. Worry not, let me introduce you to shopkeeper sparrow!'

She pointed to a nearby tree, where the shopkeeper sparrow was laying out his wares – narrow, worm-like strips of flesh. 'Beefworms!' the shopkeeper cried, 'Lovely beefworms! Packed with vitamins, minerals, probiotics, prebiotics, Omega 3! Get your beefworms here!'

The mummy sparrows crowded round. 'What are these?' they asked.

'These are worm substitutes, specially designed for a baby sparrow's nutritional needs and as close to real worms as possible!'

'So... are they made from worms?' asked one mummy sparrow, eyeing the strange stringy objects.

'Er, no,' said the shopkeeper, 'they're made from cows. But they're packed with extra nutrients and will give your babies everything they need without you having to hunt for worms! All I ask for in payment is a twig from your nest.'

The mummy sparrows weren't too sure, but what choice did they have? The expert had said they couldn't catch enough worms for their babies, after all. So they brought in their twigs, and took the beefworms back to their babies.

Over the years, more and more mummy sparrows gave up worm hunting until every mummy sparrow had to line up at the shop to buy beefworms. Their babies still grew but their nests were looking very sparse as they took more and more twigs to the shop. (The shopkeeper sparrow, by the way, had a very luxurious nest as a result!)

Eventually, the mummy sparrows had been using beefworms for so long that nobody remembered how to hunt for worms any more.

Then one spring, a new sparrow moved into one of the trees around the field. She made a nest, laid her eggs, and when they hatched, she went hunting for worms. The other mummy sparrows watched her swooping between her nest and the field, all day and night. They shook their heads.

'She'll wear herself out going to and fro like that!' cried one mummy sparrow.

'Surely it's not normal for a baby sparrow to eat that often?' scoffed another.

'She won't be able to get enough worms to feed her babies,' grumbled another.

But as the weeks passed, her babies grew bigger, and stronger, and healthier – and the mummy sparrow looked happy too! She kept hunting for worms until her babies were big enough to hunt for themselves.

The other mummy sparrows did not know what to think. Some were confused – if the expert said to feed to a schedule, and use beefworms, why were those babies so healthy when they'd only been eating earthworms? Others felt guilty – why hadn't they hunted for worms as well? Still others were angry – how could they have hunted for worms when nobody had shown them how? And how dare this new sparrow make them feel bad?

Some of the sparrows refused to have anything to do with this newcomer, but others were more friendly. They asked the new sparrow lots of questions, and she answered them all happily and honestly.

'How do you know how to hunt for worms?' asked one sparrow.

'My mother and sisters showed me,' replied the new sparrow.

'Doesn't it tire you out?' asked another.

'A little bit, but I'm used to it now, and I can rest when my babies are full and sleepy.'

'Wouldn't you rather just buy beefworms?'

'Not really. I'm glad that I can feed my babies for free, and keep all the twigs in my nest!'

The next spring, as it came close to the time for the mummy sparrows to lay their eggs, one sparrow sidled up to the new sparrow and whispered, 'When my eggs hatch, will you show me how to hunt for worms?'

And she did. And it worked. So when the next spring came, some more sparrows asked the hunters to show them how to do it. And gradually, more and more sparrows learnt to hunt again, until the shopkeeper had to pack up his beefworms and fly away.

All it had taken was one sparrow to show all the others that they didn't need an expert to tell them how to look after their babies; they themselves were the experts, after all!

Lady Seaweed

or

Tristesse

by Marija Smits

Lady Seaweed

or

Tristesse

Mathey Trewelen, why did you come a-calling?

Mathey Trewelen. His name is like the salt that clings to my lips: bitter, acrid, dead. I go about my business, watching over my little ones, but he is always here in my mind. Mathey Trewelen, gone too soon.

I call to my children but they pay me no heed, so I keep the warning to myself: *Kee-kee! Kee-kee! Be careful! Be careful!* and I hope that it gives them protection enough from unseen rocks and drowning waves.

I can't believe how big they've grown; that rock that they're playing on – scrambling onto and diving off – was too far out for them last year. Soon it'll be too close to home. I have to laugh at the humans who mistook us merfolk for manatees. My children – little waifs – are all bones and agility. And besides, manatees give birth to live young. We merfolk are more like platypuses, laying eggs and then breastfeeding our young.

Those humans tell tales about us mermaids. They cover our breasts with shells and say that we spend our time combing our hair; they believe we're enamoured of the human form. Yet none of our kind could ever desire a human, with their hairy legs and strange, cold voices – always at odds with the earth that provides for them. My children's father, my merman, all sinew and strength, is all that I'd ever want.

Mathey Trewelen, why did you come a-calling?

Mathey Trewelen, why did you have to come to my watery island cave? I was sure that no one would come a-visiting as I

69

kept watch over my eggs, but here you were, in your rowing boat, your golden hair catching the sun.

I hid under the water but watched you from beneath, my seaweed hair fanning out around me. Perhaps you saw the bubbles escaping from my mouth. Perhaps you knew I was here all along. I do not know. All I know is that you came too close to my eggs and so I protected them. I emerged from the water and your eyes shone with wonder. I had been discovered.

I told you to go away, to never return, but you wouldn't listen. You'd come out on fine days, your hair shining in the sun, and you'd call me such sweet names: *Lady Seaweed, Mysterious Mermaid.* And you'd tell me that you loved me.

But I never could have loved you; we are as different as whales and seals.

Yet still, you came a-calling, and more and more often. Then you became foolhardy and one day ventured out at dusk when the wind was rising. *Go back,* I told you. *Go back! A storm is coming!*

Perhaps my voice was lost to the wind and the waves, perhaps you heard me but chose to ignore my warning. It matters not. The boat was turned over and you were pulled under the water. I couldn't leave my eggs; they'd be hatching very soon, yet I could not leave you either. With one last look at my eggs I swam to your aid, but it was too late. Poor Mathey, weak of heart, you were already dead.

Mathey Trewelen, why did you come a-calling?

They say that he was once a fine singer. They say that he was a good man.

Mathey Trewelen, like the salt that clings to my lips, bitter, acrid, and forever a part of my life.

The Cave

by Tomas Cynric

The Cave

He woke suddenly from a sleep he hadn't intended to take. She was standing in the mouth of the cave, a silhouette against the dusk.

'We must go,' he said, raising himself on weary limbs. 'The king. We must hurry.'

'You need not hurry,' she replied.

'We must save the king!'

'We have,' she said, and then he felt the power of the dragons quickening the air. But there was something else, some other force stirring in the rocks and in the dust at his feet, and for the first time in many long years, he felt fear.

'Goodbye Merlin.'

Nimue raised her arms and spoke the words of power, and the mountainside shuddered. Fissures opened, and rocks tumbled from the cliffs, cascading down to block the cave mouth with rubble and scree and boulder.

He drew back into the depths of the cave, and let the convulsions of the mountain subside. So, he was betrayed by Nimue. He had expected as much, but not foreseen it, and that should have been warning enough, for his foresight had always failed him when it came to Nimue. He sighed, and wondered at her madness. A tumble of boulders would hardly contain him long.

When the last clatter of stone had ceased, he stood, pulled his cloak around himself, and walked through the dark to where the entrance had been. He reached out, touched the stone, and felt for its essence. His mind probed, feeling its way through the boulders, finding the truth of their form, searching for the pulse of power that held them together, named them, defined them. Then he could form the words that would unmake them.

Fear shivered through him, and he withdrew his hand.

He closed his eyes, and tried again. There was something in the rock, an unfamiliar force, not emanating from the dragons, something that fogged his mind, stopped him from fully comprehending. Something that was resisting him.

After many futile attempts, he sat heavily on the rock shelf on which he had slept earlier. The student had humbled the master.

'Merlin?'

He spun and stared into the darkness. It was a woman's voice. His eyes were not hindered by the blackness, but he saw nothing. 'Yes!' he shouted. 'Nimue? I cannot see you.'

'You never saw me, Merlin, and that is why you have failed. Look closely.'

His eyes probed the darkness, and at last, he perceived a glimmer, the shape of a woman, old but ageless. His mind worked, recalling the years of the past and future. 'Igraine,' he said at last. 'Igraine.' He furrowed his brow. 'But you are dead at present.'

'Yes, Merlin, but I have come from the Castle of Marvels; it is a gift I requested from the sorcerer.'

He nodded. 'Revenge then?'

She laughed. 'There was a time when I sought it, Merlin, and you can hardly blame me. But no, not revenge. Curiosity.' Her shade drifted deeper into the cave and alighted on a boulder opposite him.

'I was on an errand to save your son,' he said.

'No, Merlin. You were on your own errand. Nimue will save my son, and not least from you.'

'He is Arthur, Albion, the embodiment of the land, wielder of the sword of power. He needs no water nymph to guide him.'

'That was beneath you, Merlin.'

He grunted. 'I am... ill-disposed.' He watched her, and she returned his gaze steadily. The eyes that had driven Uther Pendragon to a madness of lust lay lightly on him. 'What then, is your goal?'

'I am curious to discover your nature; your true nature.'

He let a silence hang, but she did not fill it.

'Many have tried to understand me,' he said, 'but I cannot be bounded by mortal reach.'

'I know where you came from,' she replied. 'I know, because the same evil has poisoned my line since you entered my life. You were conceived in rape and sired by an incubus.'

'It is not the first time I have heard the tale,' he conceded.

'You are demon spawn, Merlin, and demonkind are forever the enemies of humankind.'

He rose to his feet. 'I have toiled through many long ages of mankind, Igraine, and ever I have toiled to save you from yourselves!'

'You cannot fully understand us, Merlin, and that is why you have failed.'

'Lust, is why I have failed! The damnable lust that infects men like a plague! Lust drove Uther to covet your loins over the whole of his kingdom, his army, and the son that you bore him. And lust drove Arthur to choose Guinevere, whose lust for Lancelot will unman him and imperil the kingdom.'

'Lust is a human sensation, Merlin. Your lust for Nimue has delivered you to me in this cave, and that is why I am curious to see if you can be saved.'

'I, saved?' he roared.

'If I am irritating you Merlin, you may leave. Simply sunder the rocks and free yourself.'

His anger died suddenly. She knew his weakness.

'You cannot, for the same reason that you failed to see me, and failed to see Nimue clearly. You are half-blind.'

'Blind to women?'

She laughed. 'In a way.'

'Ah, the mysteries of fecundity,' he mocked.

'You command great power, Merlin. You commune with the dragons that gnaw at the roots of the world and battle one another ceaselessly. You can summon the power to split rock, draw lightning from the clouds, shake the earth, or urge men on to war. You know the power of Excalibur, wielded by the true king of Albion, the clash of shield walls and the frenzy of battle that churns the greensward to mud. Such power could surely push aside some boulders?'

Silence hung in the cave.

'No? Well perhaps you sense the power that you have always overlooked. When the battle is finished, Merlin, and the notched shields hang once more over hearths, a slow, quiet power exerts itself. Roots stir beneath the mud. Green shoots push skywards. Grass spreads again across the scarred land. The bodies of the dead are cleaned by the crows, drawn down by the worms, overtaken by bramble and heath. And when old warriors return again to their battlegrounds, they bicker over whether they clashed here or there, for they cannot tell the fields in which they fought from any other part of the timeless landscape.'

'Man is master of the landscape. He learned to fell trees when all he had for tools was flint and bone.'

'True. But suckers spring again from the stump. And when the man dies, and his children forget why he felled it, the tree grows strong and tall. This power is slow, Merlin. Patient, but relentless.'

'Like a mother who has lost her child?'

'Precisely.'

'So you are trapping me here to instruct me on the nature of motherhood?'

'No.'

'Why then?'

'To save my son from you, and to maybe save you from yourself.'

'Just as you say I cannot understand mankind, Igraine, you cannot hope to understand me.'

'I know. But there are some who say that a demon cannot sire a child, that it must first steal the seed of a man. I am curious about whether you are more than half human.'

'And how will you determine that?'

'By watching what you decide to do, when I have explained why we trapped you.'

He lay back on the cold stone shelf, and folded his hands behind his head. 'Then explain,' he said.

'I spoke before of how you poisoned my line years ago, when you agreed to sate Uther's lust by using your arts to give him the appearance of Gorlois, my husband. You ensured that night that Arthur was conceived in rape.'

'I ensured that you bore a king. If I remember, you came to love Uther.'

'Are you a successful student of love, Merlin?'

He had no reply, which was answer enough.

'A child made in rape is a disturbance to the powers that you scorn, but many such children are born, and new life and new potential pulses within them, and feeds them, so that was not your greatest offence. Uther came to want the child, and I loved it as it grew within me, and so, despite his deceit and his faithlessness, I agreed to marry him.'

Igraine, or the ghost of her that Merlin saw, bowed her head. 'When you returned after nine moons, you dealt me the harshest wound I ever suffered. To pluck a nursing child from his mother's breast and carry him away, is an evil, the depth of which you do not comprehend.' She looked up, and held his gaze. 'Uther raged and threatened, and I felt as though my heart had ruptured within me, but those human tragedies were as nothing, Merlin.' She paused, and shuddered. 'But, for a demon to sunder a human child – a king – from its loving mother, that caused a convulsion in the powers that serve life. I am amazed you did not feel it and wonder – or perhaps you did, for even the dragons writhed and snapped at the tremor, forgetting their eternal war for a panicked moment.

'From then on, you have had powers working against you, Merlin. You strode across the lands directing men's fates, but forces were stirring in the deep woods, and in the mountains, and in the lakes. Forces that meant to undo the damage you had wrought. Forces that have brought you now to this cave.'

Merlin lay still. His mind, still agile – the more so now that Nimue was distant – raced forward and back in time, reckoning his failures, his misjudgements, and all the unhappy accidents that had thwarted his plans. Was there a pattern; an intent? 'Your meddling has put your son's life at risk,' he said at last.

'My son's life has been doomed by you. Your evil poisoned his fate. A child who could not learn love from his mother, a youth shaped by the schemes of a demon, a man who could not see women clearly, like you, and so loved and wed poorly. A half-sister driven manic by hatred of you and failed by a mother consumed by grief for a lost son. A half-sister who raped her brother to make another broken son.'

'A king who unified the kingdom, and will seek the grail,' Merlin countered. 'The knights may find it, and set right the errors of the past.'

'Use your foresight, Merlin. Look to the battle of Camlann. What do you see?'

Merlin looked. He saw the ruin of Albion, brought low by Mordred while Arthur pursued Lancelot in revenge for his betrayal with Guinevere. He saw the battle: the ruin of two great armies. Arthur and Mordred: a grieving father driving a spear through his son, and a hate-filled son bringing a sword down upon his father with his dying act.

'No!' Merlin cried. 'All is ruined! I must warn the king. Prepare him.'

'Look again,' Igraine insisted.

Percival! Good! Percival is with him, Merlin saw. Arthur surrendering Excalibur. The sword of power returned to the Lady of the Lake, and then Percival returning to the battlefield. Arthur gone. Borne away by the priestesses of Avalon. And in a sudden, shocking moment, he realized.

'You!' he cried at Igraine.

'Yes,' she replied.

'You have destroyed a kingdom to take back your son!' Merlin was on his feet. 'You do not care the damage that is wrought? The sword of power lost, the king fallen, the land without a king!'

'Is that what you see, Merlin?'

'Yes!'

'You are blind.'

'I am angry!'

And in his rage, the cave shook. Dust fell from the roof. Echoes rumbled in the deep.

'You cannot harm me,' she said, mildly. 'Not anymore.'

'And you cannot stop me!' Merlin bellowed, striding to the cave mouth. He reached out for the boulders, and closed his eyes. Her voice was close beside his ear.

'You are right. I cannot.'

He paused, and she drifted back. 'You can free yourself, Merlin, but your last choice, your most important choice, is whether you should.'

He stood, and listened, mastering his anger.

'A demon could free itself from this cave. You can call on that heritage, Merlin, and it will free you. A sudden, violent act can overcome the long slow burn of life. But a man would not want to.'

He watched her face. He thought, for many long moments. 'Tell me the rest,' he said.

'You see defeat in the battle of Camlann, but it is a victory. Your arts corrupted Arthur's life, either in ignorance or in thrall to your demonic nature, and that is the taint that life could not bear, and which meant he could not be the king that was needed. Our plans have led to this moment. Mordred, a doomed soul that could never live freely, is dead. Arthur, the child sundered from his mother, is at last reunited with her, and in Avalon will finally be made whole, and become aware of all that he lost in his first life. The sword of power is retaken, unable to cause havoc in the world of men until Arthur, healed in body and in spirit, returns to Albion.'

'The once and future king,' Merlin murmured.

'In command of all the powers of humankind; and able to rule justly.'

Merlin saw. His hands slipped from the rocks.

'We shared the same dream, you and I,' he said, at last.

'But you undid it, in your haste to make a king by any means.'

He sat, and stared into space, deep in thought.

'I will leave you now, Merlin. I will leave you to think in your cave.'

The shade of Igraine melted back into the darkness.

Geppetto's Child

by Lisa Shipman

Geppetto's Child

'I don't like the sounds this house makes.'

Darius ignores her. He is busy scanning the room.

They move through the rubble, stepping over the bricks and once-upon-a-time furniture: a bed, a cot, someone's long-forgotten rocking chair. She scrutinises each item, cataloguing their original use, mourning their loss.

She hears a sound. Freezes. On instinct she tries to curl into a ball. Darius walks over. Places a hand on her arm.

'Rats. I have scanned ten already. There will be more in the rest of the rooms. Focus, Alryssa.'

'I-I don't like rats.'

He leans towards her, whispers something in her ear. She strains to hear what he says. The room rocks. She clutches at his arm. Then her mind clears. She looks up at him. Smiles.

Later, she will wonder if this was the beginning of it all or just a prelude to the end.

'What's this?' She asks, picking up a plastic human-shaped figure. Holds it out for him to see.

'It is a doll. Human children used to play with them.'

'Play?'

'Check your mindscape,' he replies.

She closes her eyes and thinks about the words 'play' and 'human'. The images flow in front of her eyes. She sees small humans and knows that they are called 'children'. She watches as a small female child – a girl – pours an invisible substance from a bulbous container. Teapot. Tea party. She sees it, but does not understand the significance of the interaction between girl and doll and tea and play.

'Why did they do that?' she asks. He turns and looks at her for clarification. 'Make small models of themselves?'

'Think of it as role play. The little ones used it as a model for socialization. Primary socialization. It's the way humans learned. Primitive, I know. They called it childhood.'

'But why?'

'They used it to learn certain behaviours. They replicated the actions witnessed from their parents.' He glances at her. 'You need to find the answers for yourself.'

She closes her eyes once more. Parents. Children. Childhood. They form an image and she sees a man lifting up a little girl, placing her on his shoulders. The little girl screams. Alryssa frowns. The little girl is screaming, but she is not frightened. She is excited, happy, fearful. It doesn't make sense. Nothing the humans did ever made sense.

She opens her eyes and looks around. Darius has gone. She steps forward, unsure where to go, what to do. She wraps her arms around her waist and rocks gently back and forth. She senses movement from the maw of an open door and tenses.

'Alryssa. Come.'

Darius heads back though the doorway. She walks quickly, quietly, behind him. She wants to be brave, she wants to show him she can do this. But the moonlight shining through the derelict roof casts a patchwork of shadows onto the walls. Arms reach out to her. A face looms by the fireplace. She runs. And finds herself in another dusty, broken room.

She sees Darius beside a wreck of a fireplace. He scans the interior then shakes his head. 'Nothing here of importance. We should leave.'

'All right.' She starts to follow Darius, then stops, her foot scuffs against a dusty floor-mat. In the murky light she can just make out the differences of colour between old floorboards and new. She bends down, examining the contrast. She looks up. Darius has moved on.

She should call Darius back, ask him to examine this oddity. Instead she replaces the floor-mat and rushes after him.

She finds Darius standing outside. He holds something in his hands. 'Look at this.'

'What is it?'

'A book of fairy tales. You would not have seen one before, but I have. Scan the contents, Alryssa. You need to catalogue it.'

'What's a fairy tale?'

'I am not sure. The Others are researching their use. They are convinced they were used as an entertainment device for children.'

She looks at the images within the book. Her eyes dart back to a picture of a puppet made in the image of a boy. She tucks the book into her tool bag. Looks up at Darius. 'I'm keeping this.'

Much later she lies on her daybed staring up at the ceiling. Her Lithium cell is almost depleted but she is loath to charge it.

Darius always charged her.

The process was a complex one and involved being put on standby. During that time Alryssa was immobile. She saw nothing. Heard nothing. It was, she imagined, some replication of a human death. Somewhere in her mindscape a phrase leapt into focus: the link between life and death is a fragile one.

She thinks back to the hours spent after arriving back to the Tower. She had rushed off to her room, anxious to start reading the fairy tales. Of course she had scanned the book in the split second she had glanced through the pages. The stories were now stored into her mindscape but she wanted to experience first hand what humans did.

She wanted to read.

She had sat on the floor of her room and devoured each tale. 'Cinderella', 'The Little Match Girl', 'Sleeping Beauty'. But her fingers moved rapidly, flicking through each page until she reached Pinocchio.

The picture of the puppet who wanted to be a real boy was drawn with an artist's hand. She touched the image, tracing the strings which held Pinocchio back from his dreams. She saw the yearning in his eyes. The yearning of the loving touch from a human hand.

Now, as she lies on the day-bed, feeling something akin to dread at the thought of another re-charge, she thinks of the room with the strange floorboards. She thinks of the fairy tales. She thinks of what it means to be an android.

She hears the swoosh of the door and looks up. Darius stands in the doorway. She feels cold and something else. Fear?

He walks towards her. 'It's time,' he says.

She looks up at him and smiles, knowing that he cannot return it. *And even if he could, would he?*

'Darius, I've been feeling really strange. I want to stop the experiment. It's making me emotional.'

'That is the point, Alryssa. That is what emotion chips are for.'

'But why? Why do The Others want this? What use are emotions to them?'

He sits down next to her. 'Our role is not to question. Just to act.'

She looks at Darius, feels a rush of *something* and chides herself for feeling frightened only a few moments ago. She reaches out and caresses his face.

'I feel things I shouldn't feel,' she says, tracing his mouth with her fingers. 'Do you want to know what I'm feeling right now?'

'Yes.'

'Desire. And love. I think it's love.'

Darius scans her face. 'Your pupils have dilated. That is interesting.'

'Darius, shut up. I want to kiss you.'

He looks down. She knows he is accessing his mindscape. In her mindscape, the man would grab the female and grapple with her. They would kiss and thrash on the floor or bed or whatever available surface there was. This cold analysis was frustrating.

He looks back up. 'You may kiss me.'

She reaches over, looks Darius in the eyes. Leans in. Their lips touch, feather-soft. She leans back, looks at Darius. His detachment infuriates her.

She grabs him. Kisses him again with more passion. Her mouth opens inviting him in. Darius responds, his tongue meeting hers, circling, mimicking. Alryssa's mindscape soars. She loses herself in their kiss.

When they break away, Alryssa is breathless. She looks over at Darius.

His face is blank.

'That was most interesting. Thank you Alryssa. I need to charge you now.'

As Darius moves around her, preparing the room for her charging, Alryssa makes a howling, keening sound. Darius reassures her this is fine. The humans had a name for it: crying.

Recharged, she steps out of the Tower entrance and into the night. Darius did not wish her to go but he was summoned elsewhere. It didn't matter, she would have gone without him anyway. Right now, she was experiencing rage. She wanted to be alone.

But still, Darius had persisted. 'Don't linger, Alryssa,' he said. 'Catalogue then leave. You are not used to being alone.'

She walks along the broken roads, scanning the detritus of human civilisation. Over there an elementary school, further on an emergency room. What would it have been like, this broken city, with children teeming through the streets, swinging book bags and singing songs?

She tries to imagine the sounds but the silence is all she has known. No songbirds, no laughter. These sounds she had heard through her mindscape, as audio files, but they lacked the beauty of their creator. Alryssa does not know what she is feeling but she remembers something she once saw, a poster of a little girl arriving too late for a birthday party: she feels just like that.

She moves on, the feeling of missing something worries inside of her. It is the absence of logic that confounds her the most. Her actions were being dictated by feelings alone. She had lied to Darius, telling him she was cataloguing an area half a mile from her actual destination. Something about the floorboards in that house niggled away at her. She needed to investigate.

Certain that the action she was about to take was the right one, Alryssa presses on, but when she reaches the house, fear enters with her. It wraps around her skin and keeps her company. What she is about to do is irrational. But it makes sense to Alryssa, because of the fairy stories.

As she enters the room, she pauses and listens. If she had a heart it would be racing. But even so, her hands feel clammy and she feels sick with apprehension.

She walks towards the floor-mat and bends down. She lifts it up and rubs away the film of dust, exposing the boards underneath. It is too dark to see the distinction of colour between the boards this time, so she runs her fingers along the floor and feels a groove circumnavigating what she believes are the newer boards. *How could Darius miss this?*

Her fingers brush an indentation in the floor, like a small half-moon. Alryssa inhales sharply. *A secret door!* Her fingers dig into the groove. She pulls. It gives. She peers inside.

A ladder descends into darkness.

Alryssa searches in her tool bag for a flashlight. It was an artefact she had grown fascinated with. Darius insisted she threw it away, but she had kept it hidden from him. Now it serves a purpose.

She turns on the light. It flickers briefly, then fades. Sighing, she puts the flashlight back into her bag and positions herself on the top rung of the ladder. She should go back to the Tower and inform Darius of this discovery. But something holds her back. Some nagging voice. *My conscience?* Shaking her head, she makes her descent.

At the bottom of the ladder, Alryssa makes out a faint glow coming from a paraffin lamp hanging from a hook in the wall. A double bed is the only furniture in the room. Two shapes lie on the bed. She processes the scene.

They're human.

'How can that be?' she asks herself. 'They're not dead. They're asleep!'

She moves towards the bed and stares down at the sleeping tableau. She looks at the mother, cradling her son, her cheek resting on his, her hand curled around his.

'Are they symbiotic? No, they are the same species. Think, Alryssa,' she whispers to herself, chattering away in the almost empty room. 'Symbiosis occurs between different organisms: parasites and dogs, humans and fleas. But...' She pauses, snatches a brief look at the little boy and the mother before moving away. She sits on the floor, rocks back and forth.

'They seem different, though. He is small, she is taller. He looks fragile, she is strong.'

She thinks about how illogical this is. Humans are extinct. Androids were the only life-forms left on earth. How could this be?

She walks back over to the bed and stares at the sleeping creatures. She reaches out to touch them then yanks her hand away. 'That one is a child,' she whispers, pointing at the boy. She looks at the female. 'That one is an adult.'

Alryssa feels a warm glow spreading through her. She bends over the mother and child, studying their faces. 'They look the same. They are different but they still look the same. They are the same.'

A pang shoots through Alryssa: *I want to be a mother. But I never will be.*

What was she thinking, coming here? Her discovery should have filled her with excitement. Imagine telling the council she had found humans, alive and well, living not a mile from the Tower! She should be experiencing exuberance but instead feels utterly dejected. Her life means nothing. She is nothing. Nothing but wires and silicone with an emotion chip.

A moan escapes from deep within her as she watches the boy's face. He looks so peaceful, content in his slumber. His mother is a guardian, despite her unconsciousness. Her arm encircles her son, her face more alert than the boy's slack-jawed features. Alryssa reaches out and touches the mother's face. She is warm but she does not stir.

Logically these humans should be dead. Logically these humans could not have survived. And yet, here they are, dreaming in an enchanted sleep. Alryssa reaches into her bag and pulls out the book, frantically turning the pages. She finds the story she's been looking for: 'Sleeping Beauty'. *True love's kiss will break the spell.*

She walks back to the boy and glances down at him. When he wakes, what will he do? Will he leap up, reach for his mother, shake her awake? Will they attack Alryssa, fearing she is a monster? She does not know but she must break this curse. She bends her head towards his mouth, then stops.

Her lips still burned from the kiss she had shared with Darius. But this feeling was different. With Darius, she had felt lust and love, mixed together in heady confusion. This time, she feels...

She imagines feeling the sun on her face for the very first time. Or tasting a snowflake as it hits her tongue. It was a feeling of wonder, of hope, of something forgotten but almost remembered. It was this feeling.

It was love.

The boy does not move when Alryssa's lips touch his. His mouth is soft and warm, so unlike Darius'. Human skin felt so smooth, she never imagined how different it would be. She closes her eyes and breathes in his scent. He smells clean and whole.

A movement catches her eye. The mother is awake, staring at Alryssa, then at the boy, eyes wide, her mouth fixed in a wide O. The boy wakes up, his eyes a startling green hue. His flushed skin pales but he does not move. Alryssa is captivated by him.

'Please, don't hurt us.'

Alryssa turns her head and looks again at the mother. She has the same coloured eyes as the boy, but harder, like flints of jade in ice.

'I won't. I promise.' She watches as the mother pulls the boy towards her. Encircling her arms around his shoulder, she whispers something in his ear.

'I have so many questions,' she says, looking at the mother.

'Do you have a name?' The mother looks at Alryssa, a frown creasing her brows.

'Yes. My name is Alryssa.' She watches as the mother's body softens. Her shoulders sag and her mouth smiles a wide curve.

'Nice name.'

Alryssa nods. She doesn't know where to start. 'Who are you?'

'I'm Beth and this is Joel. Say hello, Joel.'

He looks up and smiles shyly. 'Hi.'

Alyrssa nods mutely. Her mind spins. She wants to stay. She wants to flee.

Beth moves towards her in slow, measured movements. She bends down, resting her weight on her haunches and touches Alryssa's hand. 'It's okay. You're home now. You're safe.'

'What do you mean? I don't understand.'

'Of course you don't. I'm not surprised after what those monsters at the Tower have put you through. There's no time to explain, we have to get moving. You're probably being tracked right now.'

Beth jumps up and nods to Joel. He leaps off the bed and moves towards his mother. Beth holds out Alryssa's hand.

'Come on, we'll talk later. We need to move. Now.'

Alryssa allows herself to be led back towards the ladder. She doesn't understand any of it. What about Darius? What about the council? She can't just leave them behind. It's all she's ever known.

'Beth, wait. Please.'

Beth stops and looks at her. 'You're free. Don't you get it? No more 'scape wipes, no more testing. It's hard to adapt at first. Because what they do to you...' Beth sighs. Looks away. 'What they do to you is horrific. Makes you feel as though you're one of them. But you're not Alryssa. You're one of us.'

'No,' Alryssa says, shaking her head. 'No that isn't true. I'm not human.'

Beth smiles and touches Alryssa's cheek. 'Of course you're not. There are no humans. You're —'

A sound echoes from above. Footsteps. Beth freezes, pulls Joel towards her. She looks at Alryssa.

'It's too late. They've found us. Joel, hide, under the bed, quickly.'

Joel gives Beth a final embrace before running back towards the bed. He dives underneath. Does not make a sound.

Alryssa stares at Beth, frozen. Beth grabs her by the arm and shakes her. 'They're coming Alryssa. Quickly! Help me save Joel.'

She follows Beth up the ladder. She can hear voices from two rooms away. Beth flips the trapdoor shut and conceals it with the floor-mat. 'When they find us, they'll take me away. But they will want to keep you.' She smiles sadly at Alryssa. 'You are so important to them. To us. I'm only sorry that you don't know how special you are. But enough. I need you to promise me something. No matter what happens, Alryssa, you must not tell them about Joel. You must keep him safe. Promise me.'

It was too late to say anything more. Light flooded the room as an air-sentry zoomed into view through the broken rooftop. A cruel beam of light from the aircraft shone harshly onto Beth, making her seem ghost-like.

Alryssa tugs at Beth's arm. 'Run! What are you waiting for?'

'Too late.' She points towards the doorway. Darius walks towards them in slow measured steps. Beth turns and looks at Alryssa. 'Remember what I've said. No matter what they say. No matter what they do. You have to —'

'Alryssa, what have we here?' Darius' eyes are fixed on Beth. 'Who are you? Or should I ask, what are you?'

'You know who I am, Darius. No need to play games. Alryssa knows everything.'

'It matters not,' he says, glancing at Alryssa. 'You should know that by now, Beth.'

He turns to The Others, the faceless ones that had followed him in. 'Take her to the Tower,' he says. 'You know what to do.'

The Others walk towards Beth. Alryssa leaps forward, pushing them away, holding onto Beth. 'No! I won't let you! I won't let you! She's done nothing wrong. Please!'

She looks at Darius, the android she loves and sees nothing

in his eyes. She thinks of Beth and Joel and how kind they were to her for just those few precious moments. She remembers the feel of Beth's hand on hers, the message behind one simple gesture, flowing from skin to silicone, and knows how it feels to be loved.

The Others pull her away from Beth. She falls to the floor. Watches as Beth is led away. Without a word. Without a fight. The only thing Beth does is looks hard into Alryssa's eyes and nods. Then she is gone.

Darius walks over to Alryssa, holds out his hand to pull her up. She reaches out, shudders at the contact of his skin on hers.

'Are you all right?'

Why did you ask for her name, Darius? When you already knew?

Alryssa shakes her head. 'No. It was a shock. Seeing her like that. I never knew humans existed. It doesn't make sense.'

'She's a cyborg, Alryssa. You have no knowledge of them, because they are a dying breed. When we find them, which we do, we terminate them. We cannot allow humanity, even in its most basest form, corrupt Earth again.'

'She said...'

'She said you were one of them, did she not?'

'Yes.'

'That was a trick, Alryssa. To get you on her side.' He looks down at Alryssa. 'She would have killed you.'

Alryssa blinks. *How can that be Darius? I am an android. I cannot be killed.*

Her mind is still processing this when Darius asks: 'Were there any more of them?'

You should know that by now, Beth...

She would have killed you...

'No. I found her in here. I came back to see if there were

94

any more books. She was here, sitting on the floor. I was so frightened, Darius.'

'She would have killed you, Alryssa. Remember that.'

I will remember. I promised Beth.

Darius leads her out of the room. He leans towards her, whispers something in her ear. She strains to hear what he says. The room rocks. She clutches at his arm. Then her mind clears. She looks up at him. Smiles. Later, she will wonder if this was the beginning of it all or just a prelude to the end.

As she walks out of the door something worries at her mind. Something important but forgotten. Her mindscape plays images of a puppet in the shape of a human boy, his strings being pulled by an invisible force.

The Paper House

by NJ Ramsden

The Paper House

There once was a man who lived on his own in a house made of paper. All his life he had been given paper — his parents had given him paper, his teachers had given him paper, he spent his pocket money on paper — so by the time he was old enough to make his own way in the world, he knew little else. He had left with his paper, and wandered alone till he found a deep wood, and in the deep wood he spotted a spot that was quiet. He liked the look of it, and claimed it — he set his paper down and started to make his house of it. Throughout the wood were walls that others before him had built. Once they had been grand things, but time and the weather had worn them down, and pieces would flutter between the trees. The man liked to gather them and build them into his own. Even when it didn't look right, or pages poked out at improper angles, he liked the effect and learned from it. Eventually he'd made quite a home for himself, a shelter of sheaves. It was his.

All over his house he wrote names. He liked names. Names are the things in our world, the veil through which we see it, and a good one always rings true. He would spend his days inventing them, sounding them out, and when they were good he would write them down — and when he eventually covered each sheet he would add it to the house.

When he had lived there a very long time, his house had thick, sturdy walls, and it was very warm inside even when the weather was bitter. In winter he would sit beneath his paper roof and hug himself while he scribbled, and because it was too cold to go out he would stick the paper to the inside. In the summer, he would sit in the doorway and nod his head in the sun while he lazily dreamed up names, and aired them, and jotted them down — and he would paper the place on the outside. As you can guess, the outside grew while the inside shrank — fat and fatter, yet poky and pokier.

One day a woman came along. She had been walking for fun in the forest when she found the house. She called out, excited.

'What are you doing in my wood?' the man asked, surprised to see anyone venturing near, having picked the place for its privacy.

'Oh,' she replied, 'I'm just wandering.' She was blonde and young, and the man fell in love. The woman fell in love just as quickly — the visits she made grew longer and longer, and after a while she moved in. There was not very much room for them both in the house, and though they tried hard and harder to cope, in the end the man said to her, 'My paper house is too crowded with you here.' He found her the next morning turned to stone in their bed.

This was rather a shock. He didn't know what to do, so in a panic he put her outside and worked extra hard to build a wall around her. After a time she was completely enclosed in paper, and if it had not been for the lump that protruded from the side of the house you would never have known she had been there at all. So the man tried to put it behind him and concentrated hard on his names.

The man was happy for a while and sad for a while, and one day along came another woman. She was dark and alluring, and the man was wary, but she called, 'Come out of your house and let's be friends,' and he fell for her. The same thing happened again: the woman came to him a number of times, and when asked to stay she stayed. The paper house got smaller and smaller inside, and there was barely room for the both of them, and so the man told her: 'I cannot deal with such a tightness, even though I want you dearly.' The next morning she was turned to stone. Again, he was surprised, and didn't know what had gone wrong, and because it had made him feel better last time, he put her aside and built up a wall.

It happened again, and happened again, and kept on happening till the man had such a house that he could barely squeeze himself inside, even though passers-by would think it enormous. The man was so intent on inventing names that he didn't want to care about anything else, and couldn't see round the corner.

Winters wended their ways. There came a time, as the man papered away the rocky locks of his last love, when he realised his paper had nearly run out. How could this happen? He'd always had stacks, and had not planned for a lack. The very idea had never occurred. Now that it had, he couldn't ignore it. He went inside to think.

What can I do? he thought, squirming through his tiny doorway. *What can I do, what can I do? Give me some paper, I know how to use it, but ask me to make it and I'm totally stuffed! If I'd only not wasted it walling up women!* Just at that moment his squirms got him stuck — jammed like a bean in a bung-hole.

He huffed and he puffed and cried and worried and wriggled and jiggled and yelled and bawled and swore and begged and cursed and prayed — and none of it did any good. He sucked and blew and shouted and sobbed and pulled and pushed and squeezed and squashed and writhed and flapped and jerked and shook — and nothing more came of that either. Despite his pickle he was forced to calm down. He waited for ideas to pop up... and waited... and waited again.

He was about to wait for a fourth time when a noise outside crept in. It was muffled and faint but just thin enough to slip past his torso and tickle his ears, so he wriggled his feet, which were poking into the air, to see if the noise would reply.

It did. He felt his ankles grabbed and he felt his legs being tugged. There was pulling and panting, heaving and ho-ing, and the man began to move, with the greatest of difficulty, backwards out of his box. Bits of paper stuck to him as he slid along, and after some effort — pop! — he was out on the grass. He stood up; he shook himself down. Tatters of paper flapped away on the air, some of them clipped by the breeze and wafted away, some flitting back down on the roof of his house or settling like snow at his feet. He rubbed his eyes, played with his hair and scratched his chin; and he turned round to see the sound that had saved him.

Well, well, and well indeed. Standing right there was a most beautiful woman, with ink-dark eyes that gleamed as he gazed, and a smile that crept from her face to his. 'Hello,' he said, and she said, 'Hello,' and his heart began to sparkle inside.

'Thanks,' he said, 'for getting me out. I thought I'd never budge!'

'Perhaps,' the woman said with a smile, 'you shouldn't make your silly house so small inside.' And she began to laugh because she found him funny.

Initially quite offended, the man saw her point and realized how stupid he'd been. He decided to walk away from the old house and build a brand new one — and this time he'd not botch it up, as the beautiful woman had learned a smidge about paper herself, and knew, amongst other things, how to make it. He was kind to her because she had helped him, and because he was kind — and it's that kind of story — after a while they fell in love. So they made a new house together, with plenty of room inside, and although he carried on with his naming and pasting, he was careful to put pieces in sensible places. He also built things especially for her, and learned some new tricks in the doing. He wouldn't get stuck again.

And that is almost that, except to say that so far, though that first house is still somewhere in that wood, the corner it's in is sorry and dark, and this new house sits in a sun-spangled clearing, and when winter wends it is nippy but short.

And that is very nearly that, except to say that he still lives in the house with the beautiful woman. So if you are walking, and find that wood, and go deep enough in, you may meet the two lovers — and I can't say for sure because I don't really know, but I bet from the names he's made some are for her, and they're endlessly rich — and I can't say for sure because I don't really know, but while nobody lives forever after, they'll surely be happy while ever they do.

Notes on Stories

About 'The Boy and The Bird'

Originally written for an ill friend, this piece does not pretend to any greater significance than can be seen on its surface. My intention was to write simply, without trying to imbue it with anything so damaging as a conscious "style", though bits and pieces inevitably slipped through — basic rhythms, simple flourishes, some glimpses of something other than a European tradition I might have picked up from trying to be well-read. As with its companion pieces, there was no desire to attempt to follow on from any previous well-known writer or compiler of fairy-tales — only to produce something that, like a sketch, could be executed relatively quickly, with sufficient detail and enough ambiguity in the shading to give a touch of depth and focus, in a manner that would hopefully be accessible to the general observer.

I think by the time I wrote this, I was beginning to want something more than the well-worn tropes I'd learnt from the Grimms, something more like a fable or a genteel myth. Instead of something like an abandoned princess with a cruel stepmother and magical shoes, I went for a normal boy bullied by natural forces, and rescued by a non-human being (with nevertheless human qualities) who has experienced similar treatment. The anthropomorphic animal is more Aesop than Grimm; in the latter, talking animals are often cursed humans. My bird is only a bird, but still has the power to be more than he appears. The winds act arbitrarily and won't change their ways. The boy finds a way forward after a symbolic event. He survives less by magic than by necessity, and there is no clear moral — only simple storytelling. If it means anything, that's for the reader to decide.

NJ RAMSDEN

About 'Screaming Sue'

The writing of this story was, in the voice of the narrator, 'A goddamn pain in the ass!' since it went through so many revisions.

The original incentive to put pen to paper was a call for submissions from a small press who were on the lookout for ghost stories. Various ideas for stories whirled round my head, no doubt heavily influenced by the modern fairy tales, legends and myths I was reading at the time. Late-night conversations with my husband about fantasy films and books helped a great deal with sorting through these ideas.

The voice of the narrator, with his American accent, just appeared in my head, fully formed; then the name 'Screaming Sue' popped up (highlighting my love of alliteration) and I was away. I wrote the first few lines in a notebook at a playground while I watched my son zoom down a slide.

Then life took over... I missed the deadline for the call for submissions and then I re-read the story and realized that it needed to be re-worked. A long-forgotten memory of being in Spain, and taking a pedalo out on the sea returned to my mind. I remember well the fear I felt when I saw a seaweed-covered buoy and was convinced that it was a drowned person... That incident demanded to be woven into the narrative somehow.

My wonderful husband read this new version (despite being madly busy with work) and pointed out further changes that needed to be made.

After more editing and fine-tuning, I tentatively decided it was "finished". Or as the narrator would say, 'It's as damn-well ready as it's ever gonna be.'

'Cinderella' was always, and still is, my favourite fairy tale, and although my story bears little to relation to it what I wanted to explore, in some way, was the prince's story. My narrator is rich and powerful, just like the prince, but his money doesn't bring him happiness. A chance encounter and the opportunity to prove his worth leads to him finding, and falling in love with, a remarkable woman.

The prince in the story of 'Cinderella' sets out to find his love after he has lost her, but I wanted to show my narrator doing something as (and perhaps even more) difficult: purposefully waiting for *her* to return to him. I think that we all have moments in life where we have to simply wait, and hold on, and keep faith that everything will turn out well. It can be such a difficult thing to do, and I wanted the narrator to wait, and again prove his worth. I wanted his "happy ending" to be hard won, so that he could appreciate it all the more.

MARIJA SMITS

About 'Footfalls of the Hunter'

Trapped since at least the sixteenth century in a self-destructive vicious cycle, Little Red Riding Hood has been setting out on that same fated journey again and again: entertaining, and terrifying and offering sobering warnings against dark woods and strangers to one generation after another. Her story is sometimes taboo, sometimes trite; she is patronised in one rendering, empowered in the next. Fascinated by a story so old, so well-known but yet still changeable and unpredictable, I wondered if I had something to add to this red-capped wolfish collection.

So I sat down with my computer and my imagination to explore a few things. The complex relationship between animals and humans; the difference between the tamed pet hound and the feral wolf; the comforting symmetry and the hint of narcissism in a same-sex relationship; the boundary where modern, urban life meets the wilderness of ancient forests and their creatures. I checked a few veterinary details with my veterinary surgeon wife. And I wrote my story.

I haven't read a lesbian version before, nor yet a veterinary version where, whilst the protagonist is not empowered, the hunter hero is made female. So perhaps there is something of originality here. But with a story told and retold, a story bedded deep within the oral tradition, one can never be sure.

LINDSEY WATKINS

About 'The Mother Tree'

Originally part of a novel of stories, 'The Mother Tree' was inspired by the rather wonderful Family Tree at Waterperry Gardens in Oxfordshire. It draws on the tropes within storytelling across the world of trees and apples both as positive and negative forces. The Mother Tree itself represents the very real magic of the garden in contrast with the artifice and affectations of the palace, but behind it lies the sinister power of the king with his unspoken threats and unreasonable demands.

CM LITTLE

About the 'Grief' Trilogy

The 'Grief' trilogy was written in 2007. At the time I was grieving, not because anyone close to me had died but for other losses. My father had just been diagnosed with Parkinson's. At thirty-one, my own health issues that had been present since I was a teenager were worsening. The relationship I had hoped would end in marriage had come to an abrupt and, for me, devastating end. My ex-partner wrote to me the day after we split up and told me he had found a dying sheep whilst out walking. Knowing that he had to decide whether to walk on or whether to kill it, he decided to batter it to death with a rock. He saw the experience as a metaphor for our separation. I felt like the battered sheep.

Separation was not new to me. My son's father and I had split up when he was four months old. He was now eleven years old, and, as a single mother, trying to establish a career on a very low income had been a joyous yet difficult struggle. Perhaps because there had been fractures in my own childhood and perhaps because of the chaos of my hormones, I yearned desperately for a "proper" family of my own. And yet somehow I knew that I would have huge difficulties conceiving, even if I should ever be lucky enough to meet a long-term partner — something that at the time seemed impossible. Happily, it turned out I was wrong as three years later I met my wonderful husband. However, after a barrage of tests drawn out over two years and symptoms ranging from memory problems to a blackout to Bell's Palsy to an almost full quota of conventional menopausal symptoms, I was diagnosed with thyroid disorder, suspected endometriosis, luteal phase disorder and low ovarian reserves. It was very unlikely I would ever have more children naturally.

I had just begun to write fantasy-inspired flash fiction and the enormity of the grief I was feeling was birthed onto the page, bloody and horrifying. 'Manqué' and 'Grief and the Boy' followed as I began to see Grief as a character with a life beyond the original story. Where would she go? Who would she haunt and what impact would she have on them? I began to think about the roads we do not take or that are blockaded for us by others. I came across the term manqué, 'that which has missed being', and realised that grief is often not just for the loss of our past or even the gap in our present but for the loss of the future we might have had.

Writing is always an act of translation — from thoughts and feelings to the page — but in fantasy writing that transformation can be alchemical. Through writing this series I realized that grief has the potential to destroy us but that it can also help us to heal. It is an all-encompassing emotion, so earth-stopping that it has the power to force us to pause and face up to our mistakes, to think about what we value. If we truly listen to its lessons, it will teach us what we hold dear, what mistakes never to repeat and how to mend those bones bruised and snapped by life. I believe it is our job to take what we have learned and to live it.

BECKY CHERRIMAN

About 'The Wanderer's Dream'

Butterflies appear in folklore around the world. The Maori believe that a man's soul returns to earth after he has died in the form of a butterfly and in some cultures the butterfly is a symbol of creation or fertility.

The butterfly that takes a dreamer's soul from his body and fills his imagination with fantastical notions is not an original idea. The Japanese, Finno-Ugric, and some other Europeans believe that the soul leaves the body as a butterfly while a person is dreaming. My whimsical story has its origins in a folk tale I once read to my daughter from an illustrated anthology. In 'The Dream of Akinosuke', a Japanese story, a farmer falls asleep under a tree in his garden and dreams that he joins a procession, is married to a princess, and made governor of an idyllic island, where they live having seven children before his wife dies. His long dream-life was no more than a few brief moments during which his friend had watched a butterfly emerge from Akinosuke's mouth and be taken by an ant under the tree; the butterfly reappearing just before Akinosuke wakes. Searching beneath the tree, they find a great kingdom of ants, which somehow Akinosuke recognizes as the kingdom he visited in his dream, and a small ant buried in a clay coffin, his princess wife.

In my tale, I wanted to say something about the storyteller's need to let her thoughts take flight in order to weave magic. The perception of the scene in dream and reality are a reflection on the creative process and how that is a fragile creature with wings that eludes us. It's about how finding the right words to say what you mean can be very hard. The dreamer, Vanessa (a name given to a genus of butterfly in the 19th century) is hesitant, looking for her narrative, while her friend Tanwen (a Celtic name meaning 'white fire') is awake and quick to act as interpreter of her slower friend's dreams.

I hope my little story will make readers want to spin a yarn!

BARBARA HIGHAM

About 'The Sparrows and the Beefworms: a fable'

I have always been an avid reader, and that hasn't stopped since my daughter was born — but it does mean my reading matter is generally confined to children's books and articles or blog posts about parenting, which probably explains why I've written a fable about breastfeeding! When studying children's literature I was very interested in fairy tales — how they had started out as entertainment primarily for adults, and how they could be used to explore uncomfortable topics. The idea of using a simple story to discuss a much bigger, more complex issue stuck with me.

In parenting, there are many topics that are almost taboo, and it can be hard to discuss some subjects without passions running high and battle lines being drawn. At the time of writing 'The Sparrows and the Beefworms' my main area of interest was breastfeeding, and I was fascinated by the history of how our society seemingly lost the art of breastfeeding — the introduction of four-hourly feeding schedules, and the introduction of formula to plug the gap between babies' needs and mothers' dwindling milk supplies. It saddened me that so much maternal knowledge was lost because of the advice of experts who, however well-meaning, did not fully understand how breastfeeding works.

While this story was written as an allegory of the decline in breastfeeding (and the importance of peer support to reverse that decline), it is also about the many ways in which parents can be made to doubt their instincts by "experts". The simple language and structure of the fable style allowed me to discuss what is often a very emotive issue in a dispassionate tone, and I felt it was very important to end with an image of unity between mothers. Despite the subject matter, I didn't want the story to be divisive — I wanted to retain the core message that if parents can put aside their differences, we would be surprised at how much support and guidance we can offer each other.

REBECCA BURLAND

About 'Lady Seaweed' *or* 'Tristesse'

I have always been fascinated by mermaids, and as a child whenever I drew a seaside scene it would not be complete until it had its brightly-coloured mermaid — wonkily-drawn breasts and all!

Now, my mermaids are much more ephemeral beings. I painted the woman who graces the front cover of this book in one of those subconsciously-driven moments of creativity, and when I stepped back from my picture I immediately called the woman "my seaweed lady". (I now have several of these "seaweed" ladies in my art portfolio, she is clearly a favourite!)

Mermaids then, must have been on my mind when I came across a discussion online about how platypuses birth and feed their young. Although mammals, platypuses are unusual in that they lay eggs, which they keep safe and moist in a burrow by the river in which they inhabit.

This discussion led me to thinking about mermaids... In folklore mermaids sometimes have children, but how on earth do these children come to life? I thought that if mermaids *were* to exist, they might be rather like platypuses i.e. monotremes: mammals that lay eggs. From the point of view of a storyteller, I could see the tension inherent in the guarding of the mother mermaid's eggs.

The story of 'The Mermaid of Zennor', sometimes known by the title of 'Mathey Trewelen', is an old Cornish folktale. In the story, Mathey falls in love with a mermaid who comes to sing at his church. He is captivated by her fine voice and radiant beauty. He falls in love with her, and one day as she leaves the church, he follows after her and is never seen again. Most of the churchgoers assume that he has gone to his death but later, we learn that Mathey's story may well have had a happy ending, with the mermaid returning his love and bearing him children.

I love that this old tale has a happy ending, but I couldn't help wondering *What if?* What if the villagers *were* right and Mathey had been doomed when he became enchanted by the mysterious mermaid? For how could these two fundamentally different beings truly connect with each other on a physical and emotional level?

The mermaid in my story is not an unfeeling being though, I hope that is clear, and at a moment of crisis she is put to the test: she must choose between keeping her offspring safe, or saving Mathey Trewelen from drowning. It is one of those split-second instances in life where it seems that whatever decision is made, it is the wrong one. The consequences of the decision (or even the consequences of delay in making the decision) may well haunt the decision-maker forever, causing the person, the mermaid in this instance, to feel the tristesse of the alternative title.

MARIJA SMITS

About 'The Cave'

The story springs from three of the events in Arthurian legend that I have always found unsatisfying. First: how is it that Igraine and Uther can surrender the infant Arthur? Merlin is formidable, of course, but since becoming a parent myself, this unease has grown to outrage. So, at one level this story is a revenge fantasy on behalf of ill-fated Igraine. The second event is the entombment of Merlin (variously by Nimue, Morgan Le Fay, or the Lady of the Lake). How is it that this legendary sorcerer could be trapped so simply? Surely Merlin could escape so crude a prison? Why didn't he? Finally, I have with age become more and more intrigued by the opaque nature of feminine power in the legends. The Lady of the Lake guards and gifts Excalibur. The Priestesses of Avalon seem quasi-angelic in their powers of healing; aloof on their unattainable island shore. Nimue and Morgan wield great power – far more than any mortal men. With the notable exception of Morgan (who merely visits utter ruin on the kingdom), we are left to guess what these goddesses are up to. What do they want? Why do they esteem Arthur? Are they serving Merlin or using him?

These questions stimulated the story, which served as a mechanism for softening my dissatisfaction with the legends I otherwise love.

TOMAS CYNRIC

About 'Geppetto's Child'

I have always been fascinated and horrified (in equal measures) by Hans Christian Anderson's so-called fairy tales. For these tales of poverty, self-indulgence, avarice and the dangers of lust, bear little relation to the tales we know today. Over a period of two hundred years these stories, so ingrained in many a child's mind, have transformed from a dark, social commentary into an acceptable vehicle for Victorian moral teachings. Indeed, I knew little of the real Hans Christian Anderson until I was in my late twenties. Those original Anderson tales are for adults only. Fairy tales for grown-ups if you like.

The idea for Geppetto's child came from an analysis of fairy tales. The main components of a fairy tale should include a character with a fatal flaw who after undergoing a transformation becomes a better, more rounded individual. The character also needs to overcome some kind of moral dilemma in order to achieve their transformation. There doesn't necessarily have to be a happy ending, but a profound sense of "change" should be experienced by the reader for the story to be considered a success.

I thought of *The Adventures of Pinocchio*, written by Carlo Collodi. Pinocchio is a mischievous puppet who, although grateful for his father for making him, constantly runs away and gets into all kinds of mischief, before returning to his place of safety. What struck me was the invisible pull Geppetto has on his child. This part of the original story is never explored. We know Geppetto made his son from a single block of wood. We also know that Pinocchio returns to Geppetto time and again, despite making a break for freedom. This is the theme of the story, Pinocchio's quest to be "real" and Geppetto's desire to keep him at home.

As a writer, I am always drawn to grey areas. I question the reason behind this complicit self-incarceration. Does Pinocchio have Stockholm Syndrome? Is Geppetto really just a humble wood carver, or are there darker purposes behind his caring behaviour? I also thought of what being "real" means. If you are made of flesh and blood, does this make you real? If you were made of flesh and yet acted in a cruel and malicious way, does that make you less "real"? What if you were made of plastic and wires but could tell the difference between right and wrong? If you could feel love and sadness, hope and fear?

From these questions came 'Geppetto's Child'. It is a barely-there reference to the wood carver and his longed-for child. It is the gentle probing of what makes us real. It is a fairy tale for grown ups. I hope you enjoy it.

LISA SHIPMAN

About 'The Paper House'

This was the first fairy-tale I wrote, as a student at university coming to the end of my BA in English. We were required to submit a personal creative writing project for assessment, and for some reason I found the notion of a small collection of fairy-tales both intriguing and pleasing. There remains I think a kind of warmth to such stories for many readers, and perhaps many writers — the directness of their delivery, the simple poetry of devices such as repetition, magic, and nameless protagonists who are at once the embodiment of "everyman" and vague enough to fall short of what we might otherwise call "characters". There is a fluidity and honesty in fairy-tales that makes them very attractive to the adult mind, within which, I hope, the child still lurks, even plays.

I had read the German folk-tales collected by the Grimms, and Angela Carter's gatherings of similar stories from around the world, as well as her own (subversively adult) takes on the European tradition in books like *The Bloody Chamber*. Andersen and Perrault were on the radar too, pinging ominously. My own efforts were much more modest. I sought only to present something low-key, personal, within which I hoped to capture the flavour of tradition without feeling any need to push its boundaries or make any overt statements. 'The Paper House' grew from the seeds of my early, earnest, attempts at being a writer, at a time when I needed the comforting arm of a familiar shape to guide me through its diversions. When I dug these old stories out recently and decided to revamp them for potential publication, this was the first I took to, and I am very grateful for the opportunity to now share it.

NJ RAMSDEN

Index
of Writers with Biographies

Rebecca Burland (61)

Rebecca Burland lives in West Yorkshire with her husband and their three year old daughter, Eleanor. Originally a theatre graduate from the University of Warwick, Rebecca rediscovered her childhood passion for books and writing when she enrolled in a Diploma in Literature with the Open University in 2010. She completed her diploma in the summer of 2012, writing the last of her essays with a baby strapped to her chest. As part of the Diploma, Rebecca studied children's literature, which inspired an interest in fables and allegory. 'The Sparrows and the Beefworms: a fable' is her first published work of fiction.

Becky Cherriman (47)

Becky Cherriman is a writer, creative writing facilitator and performer based in Leeds. Competition successes include being shortlisted for the Fish Short Story Prize, second prize in the Ilkley Literature Festival Open Mic and first prize in The Speakeasy Open for her poem 'Namesake', an extract of which was published in Issue 61 of *Mslexia*. Her poem 'Wolves' is to be published by Bloodaxe in 2015. After previous commissions from Morley Literature Festival and Grassington Festival, Becky is now working with Steve Toase and Imove on a commissioned project called Haunt. She has written two novels and her first poetry collection will be published by Cinnamon Press in 2016.

www.beckycherriman.com

Tomas Cynric (71)

Tomas Cynric is an academic and writer who lives in England with his wife and two children. Always intoxicated by Arthurian legend, this story collection seemed the perfect opportunity to modestly improve on a legend that arguably doesn't need the help.

Barbara Higham (55)

Barbara Higham is the mother of three children, Felix, Edgar and Amelia and lives with them and their father, Simon in the spa town of Ilkley, on the edge of the beautiful Yorkshire Dales. She is a La Leche League Leader and the editor of *Breastfeeding Today* magazine for La Leche League International. Reading stories, watching drama and daydreaming are some of her favourite pastimes.

CM Little (37)

CM Little says she has re-found the creativity that defined her childhood since becoming a mother almost five years ago. She lives in Oxford with her two young daughters and husband, trying to juggle a good family life with a job that she loves, voluntary roles and time to read and write.

NJ Ramsden (11, 97)

Nathan 'NJ' Ramsden writes mostly short fiction, preferring to explore ways of writing than stick to one thing for too long — influences include Donald Barthelme, H. P. Lovecraft, J. L. Borges, Angela Carter, classical mythology, and folktale. He has written two novels (*Nothing's Oblong* and *Scissors/Paper/Stone*) and a screenplay ('Tell Me Lies About Love', based on his short work 'Love Story'). He taught Creative Writing for several years. In his spare time he bakes, studies medieval literature, enjoys indoor climbing, and makes

music with synthesizers and a beaten-up old jazz bass. He can be found online via his irregular blog.
https://njramsden.wordpress.com

Lisa Shipman (81)

Lisa Shipman is an emerging short story writer and hopeful novelist. She lives in Nottingham with her husband and two children. When Lisa isn't writing she runs creative writing workshops for schools, libraries and art galleries. And when Lisa isn't teaching, you'll find her in a local café, eating cake, drinking tea and working on her next project.

Marija Smits (19, 67)

Marija Smits is a mother-of-two, a writer, poetess and artist whose work has featured in a variety of publications. Her work is rather eclectic and she loves semi-colons, as well as plenty of cream in her coffee. She teaches art classes at the local primary school and is a member of the Nottingham Writers' Studio.
https://marijasmits.wordpress.com

Lindsey Watkins (29)

Lindsey Watkins currently spends much of her time bracing herself against the breastfeeding acrobatics of her nineteen-month-old daughter. Her six-month-old son (birth child of Lindsey's civil partner, Sally) occasionally has a quick drink too when he realises there's a convenient alternative milk source. Although, like Hunter, Sally is a veterinary surgeon, when she first found Lindsey six years ago, it was at the end of an Internet connection 10,000 miles away in Australia, rather than inside the stomach of a wolf. In between requests for "milky", Lindsey works as a high-school English teacher and also tries to fit in a bit of reading, writing, rock-climbing and skiing where she can.

Mother's Milk Books

is an independent press, founded and managed by
at-home mother, Dr Teika Bellamy.

The aim of the press is to celebrate femininity
and empathy through images and words,
with a view to normalizing breastfeeding.
The annual Mother's Milk Books Writing Prize, which
welcomes poetry and prose from both adults and children,
runs from September to mid-January.
Mother's Milk Books also produces and sells art
and poetry prints, as well as greetings cards.
For more information about the press, and to make purchases
from the online store,
please visit: www.mothersmilkbooks.com